Also by Lois Lewandowski

The Fatal Heir

For Billie Letts,
One of my favorite writers.
Lois Lewandowski

THE BURDEN OF TRUTH

A GILLIAN JONES MYSTERY

LOIS LEWANDOWSKI

iUniverse, Inc.
New York   Bloomington

The Burden of Truth
A Gillian Jones Mystery

This is a work of fiction. All of the characters, names, incidents,
organizations, and dialogue in this novel are either the products
of the author's imagination or are used fictitiously.

iUniverse books may be ordered through booksellers or by contacting:

iUniverse
1663 Liberty Drive
Bloomington, IN 47403
www.iuniverse.com
1-800-Authors (1-800-288-4677)

ISBN: 978-1-4401-7788-0 (pbk)
ISBN: 978-1-4401-7789-7 (ebk)

Printed in the United States of America

iUniverse rev. date: 10/6/2009

For Shelley Leigh

ACKNOWLEDGMENTS

I am indebted to the following individuals for their critiques and encouragement: Laura Cooper, Stanley Anderson, Duane Morris, Dee Ritter, Janet Shell Anderson, Roger Templin, Kathy Hraban, Tonya Bolter, Tom Wakeley, Mary Thielen, Jean Lewandowski, Norma Anderson, Mary Reifschneider, Mary Leigh, Gene Lewandowski, Julie Gerber and Jean Lewandowski Curlo.

I am especially grateful to Michelle Maas, Rita and Don Adam, Shelley and Larry Leigh, Esther Wurdeman and last, but not least, Mike, Alex, Katie, Andrew and Morgan.

ONE

Some people in Bend Brook, Nebraska, considered seventeen-year-old Jessica Coffers a vicious, cold-blooded baby killer.

As Jessica's probation officer, not only did I disagree, but I had grown attached to the slight girl with the heart-shaped face who I saw on weekly probation visits. She was serious, well-mannered, and answered questions in a soft, Southern drawl. Our only lengthy conversations involved the person she cared about most: her son, Logan.

Ironically, she was on probation for leaving the newborn Logan under a bridge in a pre-meditated plan to keep her pregnancy and the infant unknown. Jessica's uncle had discovered her with the baby at the bridge and had taken them both to the hospital.

After that uncertain beginning, Jessica brought Logan with her to most, if not all, of our probation meetings, proudly reciting milestones like first tooth and first word. In fact, Logan had taken his first steps in my office. Jessica had held him upright, encouraging him to take a step toward me. I'd been an arm's length away and when she let go he placed one foot hesitantly in front of the other and then his hand had grasped mine and he'd buried his head in my knees and squealed with happiness.

It was at that moment I had changed my mind about adopting a child. Until then, I had always thought it would take a child of my own to make me complete. With my thirty-fourth birthday behind me, not to mention three years of fertility treatment, I had thought maybe it was time to just accept the fact that we were destined to be childless – but then Logan's chubby baby fingers had latched onto my hand. Now my husband, Clint, and I were thinking about adoption.

It had come as a complete surprise when Jessica's caseworker had called yesterday to see if we would consider adopting Logan. Last night Clint and I had agreed that everything about this seemed right – well almost everything – and now the case worker, Mary Lee Parker, was in my office anxious to start the ball rolling.

Mary Lee was a short, stocky woman with bulging blue eyes and a mouth that quivered when she was on point with some aspect of child placement. "We'd start you and Clint out as foster parents. It's the best way to transition in circumstances like this, when the child's been with other caretakers for nearly two years." She picked up a heavy, brown satchel from the floor by her chair and I pushed aside papers and other items as Mary Lee's briefcase came down in the middle of my desk. "There's paperwork you'll need to fill out, plus I have information on the training classes," she said.

"I'll call Clint and see if he can come over," I said. Clint worked at The Implement Company on the outskirts of Bend Brook and since we lived in a town with a population of 1,258 people, it would only take him minutes to get to my office in the courthouse. Before I could finish punching the numbers into the phone, there was a tap at the door. Mitch Banner, a square-jawed man with vivid blue eyes and salt and pepper hair, stuck his head in my office. "Can we come in?" he asked.

"Of course," I said, putting the phone back in its cradle. Mitch had an athletic stride for someone who must have been approaching fifty years of age. He was followed by his wife, Kay, who was holding the potential adoptee: a blond, blue-eyed twenty-two-month-old.

"Gee!" the little boy said, pushing at Kay to let him down. He came around to my side of the desk.

"Logan," I said in response.

"Gee? Is that how he refers to you?" Mary Lee questioned.

"He calls me Gee because he can't say Gillian," I replied. "Or Mrs. Jones, for that matter."

"But he knows you and calls you by name," Mary Lee's bottom lip quivered. "How special is that?"

Actually, Logan was anxious to be on my side of the desk because of a small refrigerator which he knew from previous visits held child-size cartons of juice. I slid my chair over to the refrigerator. "How about grape?" I asked. He nodded and watched with rapture as I took the plastic off the straw and put the sharp end through the allotted hole. I gave the juice to Logan and he backed up to me so I could pull him onto my lap. Mary Lee and the Banners smiled.

I looked toward the door, anticipating the arrival of the one thing that did not seem right about this situation. "Where's Jessica?" I asked.

"She didn't come with us," Kay said, and her eyes slid over to Mitch, giving the impression that he would explain.

"Actually, we haven't talked to her about the adoption part yet," he said.

"She doesn't know about this?" I asked.

"I told her you might be foster parents for Logan and she seemed okay with that," Mitch said.

"Seemed okay?" I repeated.

Mary Lee made a whining noise in her throat. "I thought she had agreed to it," she said as she dug through the briefcase on my desk. "Although I'm not sure if she has to since Mitch and Kay are legal guardians for both Jessica and Logan. I think I have something here about that, although family law can be such muddy water."

Kay suddenly gave a little gasp and we all looked at her. "Swallow that," she said sternly to Logan.

I looked down to see Logan's cheeks puffed out. He turned with a look of panic in his eyes, grabbed onto my blouse with one hand and sneezed.

"Logan," the Banners said simultaneously as round splotches of dark crimson enlarged on my cream colored blouse.

"Uh-oh," Logan looked at Kay and then let go of my blouse to renew his two-hand hold on the drink.

Kay hurriedly took tissues from her purse and wiped the juice dripping from Logan's chin while I grabbed some Kleenex and dabbed at the stains on my blouse. Kay started to wipe off my blouse. "It's okay," I said. "You're my last appointment for the day. Besides," I paused, "we really can't go forward without Jessica's consent." I couldn't keep the irritation out of my voice.

"Look, Gillian," Mitch said, "I can see you're upset that we didn't discuss this with Jessica, but she's not going to agree to an adoption right off the bat."

"Why, then, would you even bring this up?" Logan looked up at my face and I changed to a more matter of fact tone of voice. "It's obvious Jessica cares for this child now," I hesitated, "regardless of what happened earlier."

"You have to remember you know her personally and are aware of," Kay paused to choose her words, "of the potential she has to be a good person." She pursed her lips. "Not everyone else in Bend Brook feels that way."

Kay was right. I was one of the few people in Bend Brook, Nebraska, who actually liked Jessica. Maybe I felt empathy for her because she was one of those kids who had come from a background where the main question had been "Who wants her now?" A background not entirely unlike my own. Due to my impending birth, my teenage parents married briefly and then went their separate ways after high school, my father to the Navy and my mother to college. I lived with my maternal grandmother until I was eleven-years-old and she became terminally ill with cancer. Of course my parents had a bitter custody battle, at least bitter for me since neither of them had really wanted me.

That situation had cast a pall over my adolescence, but compared to Jessica's, my childhood had been Nirvana. I knew from doing her pre-sentence investigation that Jessica's biological father was unknown and her mother had a substance abuse problem that had alienated Jessica's mother from her family. The state of Louisiana had sporadically removed Jessica from her mother's care until she turned ten and then had permanently terminated parental rights. The mother was currently serving time in a federal prison for distributing meth. From the age of ten to fourteen, Jessica had been bounced from group home to group home until Kay had brought her niece to Bend Brook and she and Mitch had become her legal guardians.

"We have to think of the children." Mitch crossed his arms and slid back in the chair. "And I mean both children: Jessica and Logan. What is she going to tell him about his birth? That he was left under a bridge in the hopes he'd never be found?"

"Mitch!" Kay said, turning to her husband. "Don't say that! Not in front me and certainly not in front of Logan."

"Well, Kay, that's my point," Mitch's tone had turned apologetic, "Logan's either going to have to get used to hearing that or we need to do something." Mitch uncrossed his arms and leaned forward, clasping his hands together. "In my opinion, they'll both be better off if Logan is adopted. Jessica is a smart girl and she should go on to college. She could put this in the past where it belongs and Logan would benefit, too. He'd have two loving parents and a stable home. I think adoption is the answer."

"Statistically," Mary Lee chimed in, "Logan would stand a better chance with you and Clint. The situation with Jessica is another reason why you would be foster parents at first. We wouldn't want to just take him away from . . ." Logan swung his head to look at Mary Lee, who paused to reword her thoughts, "we'd want to have time for everyone to adjust."

"The first thing we need to do is talk to Jessica. I won't do this without her consent."

Mary Lee turned to me. "Gillian, you aren't," she paused and glanced at Logan, "afraid of her, are you?"

"Of course not," I said. "Jessica is a good mother and she loves this child. We need to include her in any decisions."

"Don't take that wrong," Mary Lee said. "It's just that she's always very quiet. I've never been able to get close to her."

"But you've seen her interact with Logan," I pointed out. Logan looked up at the mention of his name. He hugged the juice carton to his chest with one arm and reached across my desk to pick up a pen. I scooted my chair closer to the desk. "You can draw on this," I said and put a piece of scratch paper in front of him.

Mary Lee watched him negotiate the pen to the paper. "He's a very well-behaved little boy and I certainly can't fault Jessica on her parenting skills, but then she also has a strong support system right now in Mitch and Kay."

"It would be nice if we had more time to work this adoption thing out," Mitch said, "but we don't." He leaned back in his chair, "if we don't do something quick, the new county attorney will file new charges."

"Trent Green?" I said. "He can't do that. You can't be tried twice for the same crime."

"Are you sure of that?" Kay asked.

I thought back to the time when I'd gotten Jessica on probation. Technically Jessica hadn't been tried since the previous county attorney, Wendell Krackenberg, had charged her with child endangerment and she had pled to it. I wondered if there had been other charges that Wendell had dismissed without prejudice, meaning they could be brought against her at a later date. "Trent might be able to bring other charges against her," I conceded, "but I don't know what purpose it would serve."

"Trent Green told people during the election that he would do something about Jessica. That's why everyone voted for him," Kay said. "You know how people feel about her. They think she should be in jail. Now they're waiting for Trent to make good on his promises."

I shrugged. "I think Trent just made campaign promises to get elected. Besides, it's June and he's been in office since January. If he'd intended to do something, I think he would have done it by now."

Kay gave me a skeptical look. "We've heard through the grapevine that he's getting a lot of flak about Jessica and he said that new charges are going to be filed."

I inwardly groaned. I knew Jessica got a lot of attitude from some of the other kids at school, an attitude that was probably passed down from the same people who were pressuring Trent. At least school was out for the summer. "Do you really think everyone would drop this if Jessica gave Logan up for adoption?" I asked.

"I would certainly hope so," Mitch said.

Mary Lee took a folder out of the briefcase and started selecting papers to put in it. "Take these home so you and Clint can fill them out, you'll need references among other things." Mary Lee looked at me and one of her prominent blue eyes started to twitch. "Open adoptions are very popular these days. Jessica could still be a part of his life."

"If she agrees to the adoption, Mary Lee," I said. Logan suddenly slid off my lap and ran around the desk to Kay, putting his head in her lap and whimpering.

"He's been up since five, he's due for a nap," Kay said. She and Mitch both stood up. "And I agree with you, Gillian, we do need to discuss it with Jessica first." Kay took the juice carton from Logan and tossed it in the wastebasket.

"I see her Monday," I said.

"We'll discuss it with her before then," Kay said.

Logan whined and held his arms out to Mitch who took him and gave him a lip-smacking kiss on the cheek. Logan giggled and wiped his face before taking hold of Mitch's face and giving him a kiss.

A tendril of misgiving slid through me and I turned to Mary Lee. "Wouldn't Mitch and Kay be the logical choice of adoptive parents for Logan?"

Kay turned at the door and gave me a half-smile. "No. Our kids are both out of college and we've got a grandchild on the way. Jessica will be a senior this fall and once she is done with high school, we are done raising kids. We'd like to see Jessica go on to college and make a future for herself, but . . ." Kay's glance at Logan finished her sentence. Logan put his arms out to Kay. "We'd better get home. It's nap time for you, mister," she took the child from Mitch and walked out the door.

Mitch watched them go and then turned back to me. "Gillian," he said softly, "if Jessica is the good mother you say she is and if she really loves Logan, don't you think she'll do the right thing and give him up for adoption?"

TWO

The county attorney position was part-time, like my own, although from the hours Trent Green kept, you wouldn't know it. After Trent took office he had confounded everyone and irritated some by showing up at the Jackson County Courthouse all day, every day.

With my purse and the folder from Mary Lee in hand, I descended the steps of the courthouse to the first floor and turned down the hallway to the county attorney's office. Doris, the secretary, was not at her desk. Beyond the reception area, an older man in striped overalls with white, wispy hair was standing in the doorway of Trent's office. He was rolling a toothpick back and forth in his mouth.

The man glanced my way, took the toothpick out of his mouth, and held it between his thumb and index finger. He looked back into Trent's office. "Maybe you just don't understand your job," he said with a hint of a drawl and maybe a hint of something else.

"I understand that as a public servant, I am here to serve the people of Jackson County," Trent replied in a hearty voice that carried out into the hallway.

"Then serve the people. Don't be bothering the people around Jacksonville or," he paused, "you'll come to regret it." The man dropped his toothpick at the entrance of Trent's office and brushed past me. I went to the office door where Trent was sitting behind his desk.

"That sounded like a threat," I said. "What did you do to make someone from Jacksonville mad?" Jacksonville was the only other town in Jackson County. I use the word "town" loosely since it's unincorporated and roughly half of the residents are part of a religious sect that doesn't believe in electricity or other modern conveniences.

"He's no big deal." Trent rolled a pencil between his hands. "And he wasn't nearly as threatening as the women who were here earlier. They really have it in for that girl who left her baby under the bridge."

"Does that mean you don't?" I said hopefully and sat down in one of the chairs in front of his desk.

Trent stopped rolling the pencil and, as he cocked his head, a lock of brown hair fell forward. Despite a shirt and tie, Trent looked more like an interested student than a county attorney. "Do you have an opinion on the matter?" he asked.

"I'm of the opinion that you should tell those people that Jessica has taken responsibility for her son and she deserves a chance at life, too."

Trent suddenly sat up straight in his chair. "I never would have suspected! Gillian Jones, you have the 'L' word written all over you."

I felt a sudden alliance with the Jackson County residents who found him annoying. "I do not appreciate being referred to as a loser," I said.

"No," he shook his head, "I wasn't calling you a loser. I was calling you a liberal. But," he shrugged, "I guess it's all the same."

"Trent," I said with a patience I didn't feel, "are you trying to irritate people? Because that's what you're doing."

"You seem intelligent." Trent looked over and studied my face. I have brown eyes and a narrow face framed by dark brown hair with a natural curl. "Reasonably intelligent, anyway. So, haven't you asked yourself why I, Trent Green, would choose to be the Jackson County Attorney when I have so much potential?"

"Is it because you lack self-esteem?"

Trent flashed a toothy smile. "I do like that sense of wit about you. You know, you may be the one person in this courthouse who can appreciate this." He clasped his hands behind his head and leaned back in his chair. "In my last year of law school I started looking for something that would give me a political start. I was clerking in the Lancaster County Attorney's office when Wendell Krackenberg's decision to accept a plea in the Jessica Coffers case made the papers. Remember when Wendell was quoted as saying child endangerment was the only charge that was warranted?"

I nodded. That statement had been quoted in newspapers across the state and had even made the national news.

"Well, that did it for me. After all that negative publicity, I knew Wendell was on his way out. I moved down here immediately so I could establish residency while I commuted to my job in Lincoln. Then, I had the election literally handed to me on a silver platter. Of course, after I was elected I started to look for something that would not only get my name in the paper, but keep my name in the paper, and when I found that religious cult by Jacksonville, it was just too good to be true."

"So this is just a game for you, a way to get your name in the paper?" I asked.

"Oh, no. Not a game." Trent came forward in his chair. "This is a political maneuver," he said with emphasis on "maneuver." "This is going to get me the attention of party leaders in this state."

"Trent," I shook my head, "I don't think Jacksonville is going to get you the attention of anyone but the people who live around Jacksonville and, judging from the man that was at your door, I don't think it's the kind of attention you want."

Trent waved his hand dismissively. "Don't worry about him. I've got it all planned out. Did you know some of the people who live by Jacksonville don't have social security numbers? How can the government keep track of them if they don't know they exist? And the school they run? No accreditation whatsoever. Those are issues that would be of interest to the public, so when the media and everyone is paying attention, I'll make a public statement announcing that I intend to ensure that the laws of the land are being followed. Then you know what happens?"

"What?" I asked.

"Boom! I'll have moved up a rung on the political ladder."

"And alienated your constituents in the process," I said.

"Oh, absolutely! But you see it will just work to my advantage since we'll probably have all sorts of meetings and I'll make sure the press is invited."

"You certainly have planned ahead," I said.

Trent nodded. "Planning ahead is just one of the many assets I've brought to this job. It also doesn't hurt that I'm intelligent, good looking, and have media savvy."

"Media savvy?" I asked.

"Yes, you must have media savvy if you want to be in the public eye." Trent pulled a file from the side of his desk and laid it in front of him. He assumed a grave expression and put his elbow on his desk with his thumb under his chin and his index and middle finger resting on his cheek. "Wouldn't this make a great picture? Doesn't my expression say I'm concerned but I'm going to do things correctly because I have the best interest of the people in mind?"

If Trent looked anything, he looked constipated. "You do appear concerned." I said.

Trent sat back in his chair and ran his fingers through his thick brown hair. "See, Gillian, that is media savvy." He clasped his hands behind his head again. "If you ever have any questions on how to handle the paparazzi, I'm your man."

There was a tap on the door and Dot Derfenmeyer, the self-appointed matriarch of the courthouse, stepped into the office. She was petite, with shiny, chin-length brown hair that always seemed shellacked into place and a mouth that was far too big for the rest of her face.

Trent stood up and I followed suit.

"Dot, you are the picture of perfection, as usual," Trent said.

"How good of you to notice! I do try and set an example but," Dot paused and her shoulders sagged ever so slightly as she slid her gaze sideways to glance at the grape juice stains on my blouse, "one can only do so much."

"Can you come back later? We're discussing something," I said.

"This will just take the tiniest of seconds," Dot said, her eyes sliding down my five foot nine inch frame to my beige slacks which were patterned with dark hairs, trace evidence of a chocolate Lab that Clint and I had acquired in the past year. Her eyes stopped at my sandals which bore signs of a recent chewing by the same dog. She sighed heavily and turned to Trent. "I just wanted to see if any charges had ever been filed for the vandalism to the courthouse."

"Vandalism?" Trent said.

"To the courthouse?" I said.

"Yes, don't you remember what happened to our Easter display?" Dot asked.

"Oh, for the love of . . ." I said.

"You mean the stuff that was in Gillian's office?" Trent asked.

"Part of that stuff," Dot said indignantly, "was my five foot wooden rabbit. It is beyond understanding why someone would steal the nose off the Easter Bunny."

"Dot," I said, "it was a cotton nose and it was easily replaced."

"Nonetheless, it was a malicious act and it shouldn't go unpunished." Dot cocked her pert head and looked sideways at Trent. "I just don't think we should have anymore holiday displays if they're going to be subject to rampant vandalism."

"Now Dot," Trent said soothingly, "I don't think you have to go that far. I think you can safely have your displays."

"Well, I do hate to see that space going to waste," Dot looked innocently at me.

That space, which was half of my office, was something Dot and I had been sparring over since the previous October when Ethel, my former office mate, was forced to take retirement at the age of seventy-two. My hopes of having the whole room to myself had been dashed when Dot decided we needed to have a seasonal display in that area since that part of the room was in full view of the waiting area. "Dot," I said, "I don't think it's bothering anyone that the space is not being used. Besides, no one can even see it when my door is shut."

"That's an excellent observation," Dot said to me with an I-may-look-congenial-but-I'm-going-to send-you-up-the-river smile. "I just like to see everything put to good use and I do think my other plan for that unused area will work."

"Other plan?" I asked.

"Yes, I've already asked the Extension Office to print up some brochures and they are more than happy to do it."

"Brochures for what?" I asked.

"For the vegetable exchange." Dot gave us her horse smile. "Every summer people come to the courthouse and say they've got too many tomatoes or zucchini or green beans and offer to bring them in, so I thought we might as well just set up a table."

I shook my head. "Not in my office," I said.

"People will bring the vegetables they don't want and take the ones they do," Dot continued. "Of course, we'll provide sacks, along with the brochures for canning and freezing."

Trent sat motionless at his desk for a second. "That's a great move," he said. "You'll have the whole town behind you for coming up with the idea, but you won't really have to do anything. Dot, you are a genius."

"Yes." Dot nodded. "And now I'm off to the Sheriff's Department to see if Newt can spare a table for the vegetables. My apologies for interrupting." Dot gave a little wave of her fingers and flounced out of the room.

THREE

I usually walk the half-mile from the courthouse to our house on the edge of town. Some days I find the walk refreshing and on days like today, I find the walk therapeutic.

A little over a block away from our house is the reception hall for our church. The actual church is closer to Jacksonville but several decades earlier the congregation had decided to build a reception hall in Bend Brook. It's referred to as "the hall" and accommodates everything from wedding receptions to hunting breakfasts to the summer musical. Today, there were several cars parked in front of the hall, an indication that practice for the musical was in full swing.

Pastor Jim came out of the front door of the hall carrying a cardboard box. He was a slim man with a paunch and thinning gray hair. He wore black polyester pants with a perspiration-stained white shirt and name brand athletic shoes with neon green stripes.

"Good afternoon, Gillian," he said.

"Hello." I answered, forcing my eyes to leave the vibrant green of his shoes.

"Admiring my shoes, are you?" he asked.

"That's a popular style with kids right now," I answered.

"Yes," he said, looking down at his feet, "they are quite the rage. In fact, it's because of the youth group that I'm wearing them."

"The youth group wants you to wear them?" I asked. Pastor Jim always wore plain dress shoes to church and I hoped he wasn't the victim of some twisted youth group joke.

"They help me connect with the kids. I always say if you want to relate to today's youth, you've gotta talk the talk and," he balanced the box so he could dangle one foot out, "walk the walk."

"Do you need help with that box?" I asked to change the subject.

"No, it's empty. I just unloaded some props for the musical." The church's youth group put on a musical every year. Practice started in May and the performance was held the last Friday in June.

"What's the name of this year's musical?" I asked. "I don't think I've seen it before."

Pastor Jim chuckled. "Of course you haven't seen it! Heavens, no. Our assistant director rewrote a classic Broadway musical just for us! It's called *Annie Get Your Commandments* and I think it's going to be the best musical we've had in the last twenty-five years."

A car horn sounded behind us and we both turned to see my in-laws sitting in one of the cars in front of the hall. My mother-in-law's fleshy arm waved from the open window. "Gillian! Over here."

I said goodbye to Pastor Jim and walked over to the car.

"Gillian!" My mother-in-law, Marlene, said from the passenger seat. "Get in and we'll give you a ride home."

"It's only a block," I said.

She was rummaging through her purse. "But it's hot out and you've spilled something on your blouse. Get in, I've got a packet of stain remover in my purse and you can wipe those stains before they set." Marlene's auburn hair was pulled back in a bun and the strands that had come loose were forming small pin curls around her face.

I slid into the back seat and took the stain remover from Marlene. My father-in-law was sitting in the driver's seat, holding a newspaper in front of him.

Pastor Jim walked by and looked into the car. "Hello, Jones family," he said, continuing down the sidewalk.

Marlene waved her hand. "Hello to you, Pastor Jim," she said while my father-in-law remained immersed in the newspaper.

"Frank," Marlene leaned toward her husband and spoke in a low, urgent voice. "Put down that paper and get out so you can talk with Pastor Jim."

My father-in-law lowered the paper and looked over at Marlene. "No, thank you. I've already had my bowl of Fruit Loops today."

"Frank!" She turned her ample body toward the back seat. "Pay no attention to him, Gillian. He's never had a bowl of Fruit Loops in his life."

"Holy shimole," my father-in-law said, leaning over Marlene so he could see Pastor Jim in the rear view mirror. "Look at those shoes!"

"Frank, stop that, he'll hear you," Marlene said.

"He says they help him connect with the kids," I said.

"Speaking of kids, we've come to pick up Ashley and take her out for an ice cream cone." Marlene turned to look out the window. "I would think they'd be done with practice by now. She's been working so hard."

Ashley was Clint's niece, a leggy fourteen-year-old who had morphed from a child into a young woman in the last several months. Ashley had been selected as the lead for the church musical. Clint's sister, Linda, played the piano and organ and even though Ashley had inherited her mother's musical ability, I still couldn't picture her as the lead in a musical. Ashley was soft-spoken and shy, not unlike her Uncle Clint. "Is Ashley having trouble with her part?" I asked.

"Oh, no. It's just that they always want her to stay late and practice. Why did you think she was having trouble with her part? Did someone say that?"

"No," I assured my mother-in-law. "I just thought Ashley was a little on the quiet side to have the lead in a musical."

"Ashley may be quiet, but she's got a good strong voice. Doesn't she Frank?"

Frank rattled the paper in front of him. "If Ashley isn't loud enough, we'll just have you take her under your wing for a day or two," he replied.

Marlene twisted in her seat. "And I'll have seats reserved for all of us in the front row so she'll have our moral support if she gets nervous. And," she lowered her voice slightly, "the reason I'm able to reserve the front row seats is because Pastor Jim wants to give a surprise award to the assistant director that always plays the piano for the musicals. Did you know Scott Torrance drives down from Lincoln every single day they have practice? And he doesn't get a dime for it, either. I'm going to be in charge of giving out the award, so I'll have to sit in the front anyway. But remember, don't tell anyone about it. Pastor Jim wants it to be a complete surprise." Marlene turned her attention back toward the hall. "I hope we didn't miss Ashley. Surely practice is over since Pastor Jim has already left."

As if on cue, several kids came out the front doors of the hall, one of them being Ashley.

"Yoo-hoo!" Marlene called out the car window. "Ashley!"

Ashley didn't look our way but ducked her head and turned to go back inside the hall.

"Ashley! Over here!" Marlene leaned out the window and yelled. She pulled back into the car and turned to Frank. "Oh, dear, what are we going to do now? She doesn't know we're here."

"Mother," my father-in-law said, giving the paper another hard shake before folding it, "everybody within a two mile radius knows we're here."

"I wonder if everything is going okay," I said, "Clint and I saw Ashley earlier this week and she didn't even mention the musical."

My mother-in-law turned to me in the backseat. "Oh, that's just Ashley for you. She's smart and pretty and talented, but she's certainly not one to draw attention to herself."

Frank put the paper down completely and turned to face me in the backseat. "She takes after my side of the family."

"I wonder if I should go into the hall and find her," Marlene said.

We all watched the hall and as the other kids dispersed, Ashley came back out and walked toward the car. I watched her, amazed at the change in her appearance. A year ago she had been pole thin with freckles scattered across her nose and bangs that fell into her blue eyes. Now she was several inches taller with long coltish legs and faded freckles. Her dark, shoulder-length hair parted in the middle to accentuate dark brows and lashes.

"We thought you'd gotten lost," Marlene said.

"No," Ashley said sliding into the backseat. "The assistant guy, Scott, wanted me to stay and practice, but I told him you were waiting for me."

"Oh, honey, we can wait if you want to go practice some more," Marlene said.

"That's okay. Sometimes he doesn't even have me practice the songs in the musical. He wants me to sing stuff just to see if I will."

Marlene nodded. "That's because he thinks you have talent. Did you know he's got a sick wife at home, but he's still willing to spend time with you? That's because of your talent."

Ashley sighed.

"What's the matter with his wife?" I asked.

"Multiple sclerosis. She used to come to the final performance, but I heard she's in a wheelchair now," Marlene said.

"Shouldn't he be at home with her?" I asked.

"Oh, I imagine they have hired help. They are very well off."

"Humph," Frank said. "She's very well off. He just married into the money."

Ashley glanced over at me in the backseat. "Aunt Gillian. Are you going out for ice cream with us?"

Frank started the car and looked back at me to see what my answer was going to be. "No," I said. "I'm going home."

The car pulled forward.

"Aunt Gillian?" Ashley said. "There's something really yucky on your shirt."

"It's grape juice," I said looking down at the muted splotches.

We pulled into the driveway of our house, a white bungalow with a wide front porch. Clint had fenced the yard to give our dog, Coco, room to play.

"What are you having for supper?" Marlene asked.

My mother-in-law has her meals planned for weeks in advance and she's a wonderful cook. Clint does most of our cooking and we seldom have anything planned in advance. "I was planning on grilled cheese sandwiches and tomato soup," I said.

"Oh, Gillian. Don't you think it's a little warm out for soup? Do you have tuna?"

"Yes."

"Why don't we come back for supper and I'll make some grilled tuna melts. What kind of fruit do you have on hand?"

"I have bananas."

"Do you have any mandarin oranges?"

"I think so."

"How about pineapple?"

"I've got canned pineapple," I said.

"We'll have fruit salad and tuna melts. Doesn't that sound good? We'll see you in a couple of hours."

Several hours later I was in the yard changing Coco's water. Coco was a year old and was still a puppy at heart, especially when it came to chewing up shoes, purses and furniture. Clint and I had made the mistake of keeping her in the house when she was little and now most of our time was spent trying to teach her simple commands and convince her that, at eighty pounds, she was not destined to be a lap dog.

Coco was lapping up the fresh water when her ears pricked and she pulled her head up, drops of water falling from her muzzle. A second later I heard Clint's truck approach and Coco went wild, running to the corner of the fence in mad anticipation. I stood with my arms folded looking after her, wondering what difference she saw between Clint and me.

Coco was happy to see me but she was always ecstatic to see Clint. I wondered if we did have a child, what if the child preferred Clint to me? In the back of my mind I felt a little pang of jealousy. Clint bypassed the house and opened the gate to the yard with Coco jumping all over him. "Down," he said several times, physically pushing her down, each time a little more firmly until she sat, fidgeting and occasionally whining. Coco would never do that for me, I thought irritably. "Good girl," Clint said and Coco jumped up like a rocket at the praise.

Clint said "Hey" to me and came over and put his arms around me. He kissed me on the lips. "Is everything okay?" Clint had light brown eyes in a nicely shaped face and full lips that hid slightly crooked bottom teeth.

"Everything's fine." I suddenly felt stupid for being irritated over children that, so far, didn't exist.

"Did you hear anything more about Logan?" Clint asked.

I spent the next ten minutes explaining the visit from Mary Lee Parker and the Banners.

"I guess I can understand why the Banners want Jessica to put him up for adoption. I'm just not sure if that's the right answer." Clint said.

I sighed. "I don't know if there is a right answer." I looked toward the house. "Your mom and dad are here. Your mom is making dinner."

"I figured that when I saw their car," he said.

We walked inside together, Clint holding Coco back until I could make it into the house. Marlene was in the kitchen and Frank was setting the dining room table. Coco barked noisily outside.

"Gillian, would you slice the bananas? And Clint could you get that bag of chips down from the top of the fridge?" Marlene kept talking as we went about our assigned tasks. "We gave Gillian a ride home this afternoon. She was having a nice chat with Pastor Jim and we were waiting for Ashley."

"Did you have to work late?" Clint asked me.

"No. I just stayed to talk to Trent Green."

"Everyone is talking about Trent Green," my mother-in-law said. "He's showing up at the courthouse at dawn and working until dark. He's at work so much, he's neglected to mow the lawn and take care of the place he's renting from the Lohrmeisters."

"He's not coming to work at dawn," I said. "He gets there about the same time I do."

"Somebody at work heard that Trent Green asked for surveys to be done on the land outside of Jacksonville so he can see who owns what," Clint said.

"My, I guess that would be time consuming. He must have a lot on his plate," Marlene said.

"Humph," my father-in-law said from the next room. "Nobody should feel too bad about his plate seeing as it was a buffet and he took what he wanted."

"That's not quite true," said Marlene. "Some of it came from the people that hate Jessica Coffers."

I winced at Marlene's blunt assessment of Jessica.

"Mom," Clint said, noticing my reaction, "I think that's just a couple of people. Everyone else has moved on."

"Which reminds me, Gillian," my mother-in-law said, "do you have any exciting news that you want to tell everyone?"

Exciting news? I thought about my day and the encounter with Dot. None of which qualified as exciting. "Um, give me a hint," I said.

"It has to do with a child." My mother-in-law was spreading tuna salad on bread and looking at me expectantly.

"Ashley has the lead part in the church musical this summer?" I said.

"No," Marlene said firmly. "That would be Ashley's news. I'm talking about your exciting news."

Clint looked at me and I shrugged my shoulders. "Mom, what's the news?" he asked.

"That you might be adopting that little boy! Now, don't be afraid to tell us, we love adopted children just the same, even if you aren't getting a newborn baby."

I stopped slicing. "Who did you hear this from?" I asked.

"I heard it from Ginny Lamont," Marlene said, "who would be a sister to Mitch Banner. She should know."

"Nothing has been decided yet," Clint said looking at me.

Marlene stopped spreading the tuna. "Gillian! Don't tell me you're hesitant about adopting! You always speak so fondly about that little boy."

"It's not that," I said, stirring the sliced bananas into a bowl of oranges, pineapple and marshmallows. "Jessica doesn't know the Banners are considering putting Logan up for adoption and I don't think she'd consent to it."

"Does she have to?" Marlene asked. "You know she abandoned him after he was born."

"Marlene," I said, "she's just a kid herself. And she's a nice kid. She hasn't had the easiest life, you know."

"Oh, you're probably right. And Ginny didn't say she was a bad kid, either. She just said if the child was put up for adoption, that girl could start a new life for herself when she's done with school." Marlene moved the grilled sandwiches to a plate. "And you seem so attached to that little boy. It would just work out so well for everyone involved."

Marlene was right about one thing. I had gotten attached to Logan and Jessica. "Did Ginny Lamont happen to say how 'that girl' feels about it?" I asked.

Marlene pursed her lips. "No, actually she didn't. And don't misunderstand me. Ginny gave me the impression the whole family wants to bury that part of the past and move on. It's just hard now that Trent Green is going to dig it all up again."

We moved the food into our combination dining and living room. Glasses of iced tea were already on the round table. "Isn't it a little strange," I asked, "that it's not the Banners or their families that want Trent Green to pursue charges against Jessica? Wouldn't you expect people to consider the family's feelings on this?"

Marlene sat down at the table and took a sandwich before passing the plate to Frank. "Well, people think Jessica Coffers took advantage of the Banners. After all, they were good enough to take her in and she repaid them by getting pregnant and leaving the baby under a bridge. And then there was all that bad publicity when Wendell charged her or didn't charge her, I guess it depends on how you look at it. Some people didn't like the way Bend Brook was portrayed in the news and they feel she's responsible."

"She still should be asked about the adoption plan," I said. "Logan is her child."

"Well," Frank said, "if we want to be all fair and stuff, shouldn't that Delaney kid have a say about what happens to that little boy? He's the father, isn't he?"

I looked over at Clint who had expressed those same sentiments yesterday after Mary Lee had called.

"We wondered about that, too," Clint said. "Apparently Brandon Delaney isn't interested in parental rights and the Banner's aren't pursuing child support."

"The caseworker, Mary Lee, said she sent papers for Logan's father to fill out if he wanted to have a voice in decisions regarding Logan. She said it was sent by certified mail and he had a date to return the paperwork." I spooned fruit salad onto my plate. "Mary Lee said by not returning the paperwork, he's forfeited his parental rights."

"I thought he'd still have to pay, at least medical costs," Frank said.

"That's never been an issue," I said. "Jessica was covered under the Banner's health insurance when Logan was born. Remember, they are both minors, Brandon's still in high school, too."

"Well, I suppose that would be like getting blood out of a turnip." Frank replied.

"Still," Clint said, "I'd like to hear it from him in person that he doesn't want anything to do with the baby."

"First the Banners need to talk to Jessica." I glanced at Marlene, "before she hears from someone else that Logan might be up for adoption."

"When do you meet with Jessica?" Clint asked.

"Monday morning, like usual," I answered.

"And this is just Wednesday?" Clint glanced at his mother. "Maybe you should move the appointment up."

FOUR

My first appointment of the morning was Karl Kittman, a fifty-something bachelor with a reputation for being slightly eccentric and a penchant for being difficult.

A year ago Karl had been ticketed for occupant protection, meaning Karl wasn't wearing his seatbelt. Newt, the Jackson County Sheriff, gave Karl a citation and the directive to start wearing the seatbelt or face additional citations. This set off a battle of wills between the two and Karl accumulated thirty-four citations for occupant protection within a ninety-day period.

The tickets were combined into one court date and Karl appeared, as did the judge. The judge resembles both Dirty Harry and Albert Einstein with a craggy face and unkempt white hair. He looked sternly at Karl, held up one of the citations, and offered to accept a guilty plea for that one ticket and dismiss the rest, provided Karl start wearing his seatbelt.

Karl declined the offer.

The judge stated that the law was behind the citations Newt had issued.

Karl stated that forty-two years of successful driving were behind his steering wheel.

The judge not-so-patiently explained that when a law is implemented, it needs to be followed by everyone, whether or not they agree with it.

In response, Karl delivered a heartfelt speech declaring that no law could take away his God-given right as a citizen of these United States to choose whether he wanted to go through the windshield or be trapped in the vehicle if he were ever to be involved in an accident.

The judge thought it over, fined him, put him on probation for one of the tickets and dismissed the others. Initially, Karl didn't pay the fine. He also failed to show up for his scheduled meeting with me.

"We're going to have to revoke his probation," I told the judge. In Karl's case this would mean seven days in jail and a six-month license impoundment.

"He'll come around," the judge had said.

Two days before the hearing to revoke his probation, Karl showed up in my office, smiled, and announced that we were "shirt-tail" relation. I thought he meant he was a cousin to Clint. As it turned out his beloved Lab, Lizzie, was a litter mate of our dog, Coco, and somehow this made a weekly appointment with me fall into the category of social visit rather than disciplinary action.

This morning Karl sat across from me in faded blue jeans and a striped shirt, legs crossed and fingers intertwined across his stomach.

"You are continuing to wear your seatbelt?" I asked. The terms of his probation included jail time for failure to wear his seatbelt.

"I can't leave Lizzie alone for seven days now, can I?" Karl answered.

"I'm taking that as a yes," I said, typing the information into my computer. "You are wearing your seatbelt to avoid a seven day jail sentence."

"Since Newt's in charge of the jail, it would probably be more than just seven days," he said.

I shook my head. "Newt can't extend a jail term."

Karl shook his head. "Oh, you don't know Newt. He'd probably forget to feed me and I'd come out weak as a newborn kitten. It might take me weeks, or even months, to recover. I just couldn't do that to Lizzie." Karl unclasped his hands and leaned forward as if to tell me something confidential. "Say, I was wondering, what kind of jail term do you think that Coffers girl will get when they charge her for what she did?"

"Jessica," I said, turning my chair away from the computer to face Karl, "has already been sentenced. She is meeting the terms of her probation, just as you are."

"Now, now, I didn't mean to ruffle your feathers, Gillian, but the talk is they are going to have a real trial this time around, and then she'll go to jail."

"Did you hear that from Trent Green?" I asked.

"No. I'd rather have my little finger cut off than talk to that no-good son of a gun. Did you know I went to see him so he'd know my side of the story and dismiss those tickets since I was being profiled by Newt? Well, let me tell you, Trent and I just didn't see eye to eye."

I imagined that was the understatement of the year. "I think Trent has his priorities and it probably didn't matter to him if your tickets were dismissed," I said.

Karl nodded. "Well, that's true. He thinks he has bigger fish to fry but, mark my words, that kid is too ambitious for his own good. He'd better back off or it's going to catch up with him one of these days."

"So," I said, crossing my arms and rocking back in my chair, "are you saying Trent should drop the matter with Jessica?"

"Well, I'd have to think about that. That was a pretty heartless and cruel thing that girl did and I witnessed it firsthand."

I stopped rocking. "What do you mean, you witnessed it firsthand?"

"I came across them at the bridge, remember? I was coming up over the hill in my truck and there was Mitch standing in the ditch, holding the baby. His mouth was so far open, it could have hit the ground."

"Wait, it was Mitch who found Jessica and the baby at the bridge," I said, holding my hand up and trying to remember the details as I had heard them nearly two years ago. "Where was Jessica?"

"She was there, too," Karl said. "Jessica was in the car."

"The car?" I asked. "As in Mitch's car?"

"There was only one car there and it must have been Mitch's," Karl said.

"Wouldn't there be two vehicles since Mitch found her at the bridge and then you came along and found them both?"

"You know, now that I'm thinking back about it, Newt asked me that very same question but not nearly as quick. I think you've got the wrong job here, you oughta be the one with a badge."

I turned around to shut my window air conditioner off. "Karl," I said, "tell me what happened when you found Mitch and Jessica at the bridge."

"Well, from what I remember, it seems that Jessica had left the baby at the bridge and then gone home to clean up but Mitch saw her and I'm guessing there was blood and whatnot on her clothes because then she told him what she'd done. Then I guess he whisked her into the car and they took off for the bridge to get that baby. And that's when I came across them. Mitch put the baby on the front seat of the car and off they took for the hospital."

"Ahhh," I said. No wonder Wendell had only charged Jessica with neglect. She had participated in the rescue, so to speak. I wondered if Trent was aware of that fact.

"Gillian?" Karl asked.

"I'm sorry," I said, "I was lost in thought."

"Well you can go back to your thinking because I told Lizzie I wouldn't be more than forty-five minutes and she's in the pickup waiting for me."

If I didn't know Lizzie was a dog, I would never guess Lizzie was a dog from the way Karl talked about her. "I'll see you next Thursday," I said and flipped open my calendar. "Wait, that won't work. I've already got an appointment next Thursday at 8:30. Someone rescheduled since the Fourth of July is on a weekday."

Karl stood up and put his seed cap on his head. "Can we make it Monday instead?"

"Same time?" I asked.

"Yep. I'll be here at 8:30 on the button. And I'll bring you something for your table." He stood up and indicated the table in the corner which had a stack of brochures strewn across it and a piece of paper taped to the side, which someone had written in black marker VEGETABLE EXCHANGE.

"It's not my table," I said.

"Well, I should think not, as dusty as it is, and look at those spider webs underneath it. Tell you what, you get that table cleaned up and I'll bring you some of my new red potatoes," he said and walked out the door.

"It's not my table," I said to the empty room. I tapped my pen on the desk a few times and then got up and turned around to the window air conditioner behind my desk and moved the knob to freezer mode. The courthouse had window air conditioners and mine either worked too well or not at all. From where I stood at the window, I could see the street behind the courthouse. Lizzie was in the truck bed of Karl's pickup, her eyes pinned to me in the second story window. Had she known Karl had just been in my office? No, of course not. She'd just noticed movement at this window, that was all. Her tail wagged slightly and she turned her gaze to the side of the courthouse where Karl soon appeared. She gave several barks and then looked back up at me. Karl followed her gaze and waved. I lifted my hand in response, a chill working its way up my spine. Dogs can't communicate, she couldn't have known that Karl was in my office.

I shut off the air conditioner and heard a sound behind me. I turned and gave an involuntary gasp. Bob Johanson, a man I knew from church, was sitting in one of the chairs on the other side of the desk. He looked terrible. His large blue eyes were prominent in a gaunt face, thin patches of white hair hung with no discernible pattern to the top of his otherwise bald head and his clothes hung on him. I knew from Pastor Jim's prayer requests that Bob had cancer, but the change in his appearance was startling.

"Bob," I recovered my shock and leaned forward to offer my hand. "What a surprise to see you here."

Bob shook my hand with a firmness I found remarkable in such a frail looking individual. "I heard yesterday you were going into the vegetable business so I brought you some radishes," Bob pointed toward the table.

"Thank you," I replied. Dot and I needed to have a little talk.

"But that's not the real reason I came."

"Oh?" I said.

"Howard Mehrman says you are good at figuring things out and I have something I want you to investigate."

I sat down at my desk across from Bob. My career after college had consisted of working for a private investigator that specialized in missing persons, a dramatic way of saying he found people who didn't pay their bills. Because of that previous job, county commissioner Howard Mehrmam, along with my mother-in-law and the judge, had helped implement an investigation "job" for me in Colorado the previous year. That job had nearly cost me my life. "Bob," I said, "Howard hired me to work in Colorado, I didn't have to be licensed there."

"Howard told me he hired you to get things right with his daughter and I want to hire you on account of my youngest child, my only daughter," Bob continued.

Bob had two sons that lived in Bend Brook. "I didn't know you had a daughter."

"She was my youngest," he repeated. Bob leaned forward slowly and fumbled in the back pocket of his jeans until he brought out a billfold. He opened it and flipped through plastic dividers, then with trembling hands held it toward me. A gold embossed '84 winked from the bottom corner of the picture and I took the wallet so I could get a closer look at the girl with light brown hair. She stood at the base of a tree that divided and sent separate trunks skyward. Her head was turned so she smiled directly into the camera. She was slender and pretty and exuded a certain confidence and wholesomeness that I didn't usually see in my juvenile probation clients.

"Very pretty," I handed the picture back.

Bob smiled. "She took after her mother in looks which was lucky for her."

I had never seen Bob's wife at church. "Your wife is gone?" I asked.

He nodded. "My wife died when JoJo was seven-months-old."

"JoJo?" I asked.

"My daughter. We named her Rebecca, but after she was born, one of the boys, Russ I think it was, said 'welcome home Rebecca Jo Johanson' and she started to cry. He picked her up and said 'what's the matter JoJo?' and she was JoJo ever after. About a year or so later that Beatles song came out about JoJo and people would ask us if we called her that because of the song." His dry lips stretched into a smile. "The boys would get indignant and say that she had the name first."

He continued to look at the picture. "Everybody around here always called her JoJo. It was how she was listed at school and church and 4-H. Nobody ever called her Rebecca until she went to college."

"Where did she go to college?"

"UNL."

The University of Nebraska at Lincoln was only a couple of hours from Bend Brook. I had graduated from UNL with a double major in Criminal Justice and Political Science. "What was her major?"

Bob's smile faded. "JoJo dropped out in her second year of college because, well, the because of it all is what I want you to look into."

My smile faded. "You want me to find out why your daughter dropped out of college?"

"No, I think I know the reason she dropped out. This is hard for me to say but when JoJo, Rebecca that is, was a sophomore in college a man tried to rape her. I want to know who it was."

"Bob," I said slowly, "this is, or was, a police matter. Did your daughter contact the police when it happened?"

"Yes, but you see, her roommate came home and the man left so they never considered it a real crime since nobody was hurt. At least, nobody was physically hurt."

"Wouldn't they have investigated it as a break-in?"

"I don't think they even did that because there was no break-in. He knocked at the door and she answered."

I looked across my desk at Bob's sunken eyes. "Bob," I said gently, "a crime that happened," I did a quick calculation, "over twenty years ago would be nearly impossible to solve. There would be nothing to go on." I shook my head. "And you couldn't begin to narrow down a suspect."

Bob leaned forward in his chair. "You could narrow it down to someone from Bend Brook."

"Why do you think it's someone from Bend Brook?" Bend Brook residents on the whole are generally a good group of people, even if some of them were on the vindictive side about Jessica Coffers. Most were trusting enough to leave houses and cars unlocked, and more than willing to help out their friends and neighbors.

Bob slowly put the billfold back in his pocket. "When JoJo went to college she went by the name Becky. She told me she was going to use the name Rebecca or Becky because JoJo sounded like someone's pet dog. Her roommates called her Becky, her professors called her Becky or Rebecca, everyone there knew her as Becky or Rebecca. And then that night, the night that it happened, her roommate came home and found this man holding a knife to JoJo's throat and the man said 'Don't move, JoJo, or I'll kill you.'"

"My God, Bob, was she hurt?"

"No, her roommate screamed and he ran. It's the only good thing that roommate of hers ever did. I personally blame the roommate for the whole thing to begin with because she worked at some stripper bar which probably gave someone the wrong idea."

I shook my head for a second to disagree until I saw Bob's eyes again. "Bob, maybe you should ask JoJo how she feels about having this revisited."

Bob took a raspy breath. "I forget you haven't lived here that long. JoJo was killed in a car accident in 1994."

"I didn't know. I'm sorry to hear that."

"You'll do it then? You'll look into this for me?"

"Well," I paused and picked up my desk calendar and opened it. I would have to tell Bob it just wasn't feasible and that I didn't have time. I heard a slight slap on my desk. Bob had laid a checkbook down and was writing a check out in spidery handwriting.

"Bob," I said. He looked up and his big blue watery eyes met mine. "I can't accept a check from you. It would be illegal for me to take money from you. I'm not a licensed investigator in Nebraska."

"Would you look into for me as a friend?" Bob asked. "There shouldn't be nothing illegal about that."

"Well," I paused. "I guess I could check into it, but I really doubt there's anything to find after all this time."

"But you'll do it?"

I sighed. "Don't get your hopes up. I don't think it will amount to anything."

He didn't move right away but then ever so slowly the checkbook was withdrawn and put in his shirt pocket. He looked at me and nodded. "Fair enough. But please, Gillian, make it a priority. This is something I need to know."

After Bob left, I folded my arms and put my head down on my desk. I heard footsteps at the door of my office, heavy footsteps. Footsteps that, thankfully, did not sound like Bob's. I lifted my head up. It was the judge, standing in the doorway with a cup of coffee.

"I heard Bob Johanson was up to see you," the judge said, grimly taking a seat in the chair Bob had recently vacated. "Bob asked me a couple of weeks ago if I'd thought you'd make a good investigator and I told him that you were not pursuing that line of work."

"Bob must have forgotten that conversation because he wants me to look into his daughter's attempted rape."

The judge slurped some coffee. "How terribly difficult it must have been for you to tell him no."

I winced.

The judge set his cup down on the desk. "You did tell him no, didn't you?"

"I told him I'd check into it. I wanted to tell him it was hopeless, but I just couldn't."

The judge's eyebrows moved together in deep concentration. "That was a good answer. Bob needs to have hope somewhere in his life right now."

"That might be true, but his daughter's been dead for over ten years. You would think he'd have at least reconciled himself to this after she died."

The judge picked his coffee cup up. "I think it was Faulkner who said, 'the past is not dead. In fact, it's not even past.'"

I leaned back in my chair and crossed my arms. "Did Faulkner ever say anything helpful? Maybe something about where you'd start with a case that is both dead and past?"

The judge put his coffee cup down and his hands formed a steeple in front of his massive frame, a gesture that indicated either he's pleased or, as in the immediate instance, deep in thought. "You could talk to some of the people who knew JoJo. Two of Bob's sons live in Bend Brook."

"And Bob said she had a roommate," I said.

"Yes, but it's hard to say where she'd be at by now. If I remember correctly, Bob detested this particular roommate but JoJo must have been very close to her. I'd talk to the boys and see if anything comes together in their minds. I don't think it will, mind you. But at that point I think you could tell Bob in good faith that you've checked, there are no leads, and he'll just have to leave it in God's hands. Speaking of which," the judge picked up his coffee cup, "I'll be seeing Pastor Jim at coffee this afternoon and I'll put a bug in his ear that Bob is still unsettled about JoJo."

"You're having coffee with Pastor Jim?" I asked. Somehow Pastor Jim and the judge had never crossed in my mind as bosom buddies.

The judge took a sip of coffee. "He goes to the penitentiary in Lincoln for a Bible study on the fourth Tuesday of every month. One of the inmates had a legal question."

"Oh," I said and wondered what Pastor Jim wore that might help him relate to the prisoners.

"Knock, knock," my mother-in-law's voice sang from the doorway. She looked in and saw the judge and her hand went to her mouth. "I'm interrupting a meeting!"

"No, not at all Marlene," the judge assured her. "It's motion day in Gage County and I need to be on the road."

The judge made his way out the door as my mother-in-law fluttered over to the produce table in the corner. "I was just dropping off pies at Gap's and Bob said he'd come by with radishes." Gap's was the town's bar and restaurant.

Marlene looked at the brochures. "Do you have any lettuce yet? There is nothing better then a wilted lettuce salad. And the lettuce is liable to wilt on its own in this heat." My mother-in-law fanned her face with one of the brochures left by the extension staff.

As a probation officer, I have access to the Nebraska Criminal Justice Information System and the National Crime Information Center, but when I really want to know everything about a resident of Bend Brook, I have a much more extensive resource: my mother-in-law. "Marlene," I said, "did you know Bob Johanson's wife?"

"Ruth Johanson? Of course I knew her. Linda and the Johanson's third oldest boy are the same age.

"I thought there were just two sons," I said.

"No, there are four boys. Rob's the oldest. He farms his dad's land and bought the house and buildings that used to belong to Eli Tenbetter. That was a good move for Rob because it's right next to the Johanson home place."

I vaguely knew Rob from seeing him at church and around town. Rob was a tall, lean version of his father. "And Russ is next?" I asked.

"Russ is the youngest boy. There's two more between them. Ron is the second oldest; he married a girl from Idaho and they live in Seattle. Reggie is next and he's married and lives in Syracuse, New York." She settled in the chair across from me. "And then there's Russ."

Russ sold insurance in a building on the other side of the square from the courthouse. He also had a real estate license and handled some of the property transactions in Bend Brook. Shorter and stockier than his father and brother, Russ was a friendly guy who always said hello to me when he was in the courthouse.

"Russ is pretty nice," I said.

Marlene nodded. "He's just like his mother, always a smile and a kind word for everyone. Ruth would be so proud of him. It was such a tragedy when she died."

"And JoJo was just a baby," I said.

"JoJo was with her when it happened," Marlene said. "It started out to be just a typical morning, the boys were off to school and Bob went out to do chores while Ruth fed JoJo. When he came back in, JoJo was sitting in her high chair and Ruth had collapsed. She'd been feeding JoJo and she still had the baby spoon in her hand." Marlene shook her head. "Bob called for the rescue unit and they got Ruth to the hospital but she'd had an aneurysm. She'd been having headaches, but not so bad that she'd gone to see a doctor or anything. They told Bob it had just been a time bomb waiting to go off and when it did, that was it."

"That must have been terrible for the children," I said.

"It was, but you know, they were a close family. And Bob and those boys took care of JoJo like you wouldn't believe. Of course, Russ would have been around eight when she was born and Rob would have been about thirteen or maybe fourteen so it wasn't like Bob was left with a bunch of little ones. But those boys all chipped in and took care of JoJo. Especially Russ. Why, I remember one summer when Russ was about ten, he went to camp and was supposed to be gone for a week, but he called and had his dad come get him after three days because he was just so homesick for JoJo."

I thought of JoJo's high school picture. "She did seem to come out of everything okay. Except maybe for the attempted . . ." I stopped in midsentence. Would JoJo's situation at college have been common knowledge in Bend Brook?

"You mean that attack on her at college?" Marlene lowered her voice. "It wouldn't have happened if she would have had a decent roommate." She lowered her voice even further. "The roommate worked at a topless bar and I've always agreed with Bob, she was just no good."

Marlene was usually quick to offer her opinion but usually her opinions weren't so judgmental. "How can you be sure she was no good? You didn't even know her."

Marlene straightened her shoulders. "Bob told me she was trash and I knew he was right when I saw her at JoJo's funeral."

"You decided this at a funeral?"

"Oh, Gillian, you should have seen her! It was the dead of winter and she came to the funeral with jet black hair that was spiked this way and that, and she wore these black leather boots and a short white dress with a black belt that just hung on her hips. And worst of all, you could tell she had on black underwear underneath! Now, I'm not Emily Post, but I don't need someone to tell me you don't wear white in winter, especially not to a funeral, and you don't wear white anytime with colored underwear." Marlene lifted her chin. "And I am talking all of her underwear, not just her panties."

I shrugged. "I doubt if her roommate's choice of clothing had anything to do with JoJo's assault."

"You never know. Women are attacked right and left in the big city. It's not like Bend Brook."

"Marlene," I said, "Women are not attacked right and left. I went to college in Lincoln, too. I would have started a couple of years after JoJo dropped out. I'm not saying it doesn't happen, but it's not a daily occurrence."

"Now, Gillian, you drove back and forth to Omaha and lived at home which was probably a very good idea. In fact, I was just talking to Georgia Lohrmeister not too long ago, and she was telling me about how well her daughter, Brenda, is doing. Brenda is a manager of a chain of clothing stores in Kansas City. Anyway, you know Georgia is one of my best friends, and

I'm sure you won't say anything, but Brenda was, you know, attacked when she went to college. That would have been a year or so before JoJo was attacked."

"Attacked? As in raped?" I asked.

Marlene held up a hand, "yes, but you absolutely can't say anything. It's a very sensitive subject with Georgia."

"Where did this happen?" I asked.

"In Lincoln. Brenda was attending the university."

I shook my head. "It's just a coincidence."

Marlene leaned forward. "Well, is it a coincidence that it happened to Marge Kittman's daughter, too? And that she was in Lincoln at college when it happened? Although you absolutely cannot say one word about Marge's daughter. Very few people know about it and she prefers to keep it that way."

"Marlene, when did this happen to Marge's daughter?" I asked.

"Well, let me think, she was a bit younger than both JoJo and Linda. Oh, I know! It would have been eighteen years ago because I was baking a cake for Josh's baptism when Marge Kittman called about Denise." Josh was Clint's nephew.

"Were either Denise or Brenda's assailants ever caught?"

"Now that you mention it, no, I don't think they were. At least not Brenda's because Georgia would have told me. And Gillian, remember, you can't say a word about Marge's daughter. Or Brenda for that matter. Why are you asking about all this?"

"It just seems so odd that it would happen to three women from Bend Brook. Do you know if JoJo got a good look at the person?"

"I really couldn't tell you that, either. I don't know if anyone could now that JoJo's gone."

"Marlene," I said. "do you remember the name of the roommate that came to the funeral?"

"Let's see, it was a different name. It was a summery name, like her dress. Even though the dress did have long sleeves.

"You were introduced to her, then?"

"Not really. She asked me where she could leave the plant she had brought and I took it to the funeral director. It was a white poinsettia."

"A white poinsettia? That is different for a funeral."

"Well, it was the holiday season. JoJo died the day after Christmas."

"Poor Bob," I said. "He lost his wife and his daughter."

Marlene pursed her lips. "I think he'll be seeing them soon enough. By the looks of him, Bob Johanson isn't long for this world."

FIVE

Make it a priority had become a refrain in my thoughts ever since Bob had left my office. I tapped my pen on my desk and checked the time. It was nearly noon, I should be leaving, except I had told Bob I was going to look into the attempted attack on JoJo and I needed to think of something I could do.

I sighed. I couldn't talk to JoJo and I doubted if any police report still existed for a crime that hadn't happened. Of course, I could talk to Russ and see if he had any more information on the roommate besides her "summery" name and inappropriate underwear. And what about those other girls? My pen stopped in mid-tap. If I could get the investigative reports on the other women who had been raped, I'd have a description of the attacks and the rapist. If I could find JoJo's roommate, I'd be able to find out if there were any similarities.

Obtaining police reports that were decades old would be difficult and I knew I would need help. I left my office, walked down the steps and turned down the hallway to Trent Green's office. Trent had clerked in the Lancaster County Attorney's office. He might know how to get the reports, if they still existed.

Doris, a sixtyish woman with styled gray hair, was sitting at the desk in the reception area. "Is he in?" I asked.

She sighed, looked at her watch, and nodded. "Do you want me to tell him you're here?"

"Doris, who is it?" Trent asked from his office.

"Gillian Jones," Doris replied.

Trent came and stood in the doorway. He crossed his arms and cocked his head. "Can you get rid of her? She just wants to harass me about the Coffers girl." He winked at Doris.

A smile played on Doris's usually serious face. "No, you'll have to get rid of her yourself," she replied, "it's time for me to leave."

"Actually," I said, "I'm here to ask a favor. It doesn't have anything to do with Jessica."

"Hallelujah!" Trent unfolded his arms. "Doris and I have about had it with opinions on what should be done with the Coffers case."

Doris turned to look at her boss. "Not only have I had it, but I should have left thirty minutes ago. It is alright that I leave, isn't it?"

"Oh, yes. Go ahead. And thank you, Doris." Trent turned and went into his office. "Come on in, Gillian." He sat down in the chair behind his desk.

I sat down at one of the chairs in front of his desk. "It sounds like you and Doris had a tough morning."

Trent waved his hand dismissively. "It's all said and done. Now, tell me about this favor. I'm already looking forward to a bit of a diversion."

"I need to find some police reports that are about twenty years old," I said.

Trent started to get up. "Just a second and I'll call Doris back. We've got a back room full of old files and she'll know where to find them."

"No, no," I hurried to explain, "these reports would be from Lancaster County."

"Oh." Trent sat back down in his chair. "And what kind of report?"

"Reports." I said. "They were sexual assaults."

"Prosecuted and convicted?" he asked.

I hesitated. "No, I'm not sure if any suspects were identified, much less arrested."

"You said Lancaster County. Do you mean the county or are these within Lincoln city limits?" Trent asked.

"I believe they were within city limits," I replied.

"Were the victims adults or children?"

I thought for a moment. "They were young, adult women."

"Then you'd probably want to start with Records Division at the Lincoln Police Department. The reason I asked about the age is because if the victims had been children, there is no statute of limitations. However, the statute of limitations is seven years if the sexual assault victim is an adult. I don't know what their policy is for keeping evidence for crimes that are past the statute of limitations. I do know their evidence room was flooded a couple of years ago." Trent rolled his pen back and forth between his palms and pursed his lips together. "I have a friend who works at LPD and if you give me the victims names and an approximate date of the offense, I could have him check it out for you."

"That would be great." I took a sticky note from a dispenser on his desk and started writing down the names. What had the Lohrmeister girl's first name been? Barbara. No, Brenda. That was it. And the other girl was Denise Kittman.

Trent took the piece of paper from me, read the names and dates and then laid it down on the desk between us. He leaned back in his chair, hands behind his head. "And why do you want these old reports?"

"The victims are all from Bend Brook and I want to see if there were any similarities in the assaults."

Trent's hands came down from behind his head and he pulled forward in his chair. It took him a moment before he could express his thoughts. "You're looking for a serial rapist?"

I pushed the piece of paper at him. "No. And just to make sure you understand, I'm going to say it again: No! I think it's probably just coincidence that all the women are from Bend Brook. It was something," I paused, "that I came across and wanted to check out."

"I'm certainly glad you came to me. A sexual predator targeting Bend Brook would certainly make headlines.'"

"Trent," I said firmly, "this is not going to make any headlines. It's probably just coincidence, nothing more."

"Gillian," Trent leaned across his desk, "I see potential here. I think we need to start a good old boy network."

"A good old boy network?" I asked.

"Sure. You scratch my back and I'll scratch yours. Politicians do it all the time."

"I'm not a politician," I said, "and I don't scratch."

"Okay, then, let's call it a deal. If the police reports exist, I'll get them for you. I'll even go one step further and see if any evidence was kept in the event it can be tied into cases that are not beyond the statute of limitation."

"These case are old . . ."

Trent pointed his pen at me. "Let me finish. In exchange for doing that, I want two things from you. Deal?"

I hesitated. "That would depend on the two things that you want from me." I didn't like where this was going.

"First, you have to share the information with me. If you find that a serial rapist was preying on the women of Bend Brook, the impact for me could be huge. That is just the sort of thing the public loves. Of course, the statute of limitations would have run but I'd find another angle to bring it forward."

I held my hand up in a 'halt now' gesture. "There's a problem with that," I said. "The women in question don't know I'm checking this and probably don't want it 'brought forward.' And I want to remind you again that it's probably just coincidence and nothing more."

"Gillian," Trent said in his holier-than-thou voice, "you know I would treat any evidence with the utmost tact and consideration for the victims. And if it turns out to be nothing," he shrugged his shoulders, "then it turns out to be nothing. I understand this is a 'maybe' situation."

"Was there another part to the deal or was that it?" I asked.

"The second part will be a snap for you. I want someone to do legal research for me and I want you to convince Howard Mehrman that creating an intern or law clerk position is a good idea."

Howard Mehrman was the county commissioner who had been responsible for the start and end of my career as an investigator the previous fall. Howard still stopped by my office on his frequent trips to the courthouse to visit and offer some advice on raising Coco. "Why don't you ask Howard yourself?" I said.

"I don't think Howard would listen to me, but he would listen to you. All you'd have to do is bat your eyelashes and say 'Howard, I think it would be a good idea to have an intern helping Trent,' and then he'll talk the other two county commissioners into agreeing to it."

"I don't bat my eyelashes," I said. "Besides, you have Doris. She's more than capable."

"Doris is capable of filing and answering the phone. I want someone who will do legal research for me." Trent emphasized the words "legal research" as if that would make the concept understandable. "All you have to do is tell Howard you think it's a good idea. One little sentence. After that he can do what he pleases, but I know Howard likes you and if he hears you say it's a good idea, I think he'll go for it. And if he goes for it, then the other county commissioners will follow and it will be a done deal."

"But . . ." I said.

"But," Trent held up his index finger, "if Howard says no, he doesn't want to create the position, then that's how it will be. Certainly that can't be too compromising for you, can it?" He leaned across the desk. "What do you say, Gillian? Do we have a deal?"

I fidgeted in the chair. "Howard may not like the idea."

"That's true. And, as I stated before, I may not be able to come up with those police reports. We'll both be taking a chance here."

In my mind I heard Bob's voice asking me to make it a priority. "Okay, we have a deal."

Trent picked up the piece of paper from the middle of his desk and put it in his shirt pocket.

I stood up. "How soon do you think it would be until you know about the police reports?"

"Police reports?" questioned a voice behind my chair. I turned to see Trudy March. Trudy was a tall, angular woman who always seemed to rub me the wrong way. She was the most outspoken critic of Jessica Coffers and, to make matters worse, she had a daughter in Jessica's class. Clint told me I should just take deep breaths and walk away from her when she started to talk about Jessica. I took a deep breath.

Trudy pointed a finger at Trent. "It's about time you took a look at those reports so you can see just what that girl did and why she should be behind bars instead of walking around town any which way you please."

"Yes, I was just saying that I needed to see those reports," Trent said heartily, as he got up out of his chair and put out his hand.

Trudy did not take the proffered hand. "I came over here because I just heard that you waffled on your campaign promise to fix the situation with the Coffers girl. I am here to remind you that the only reason I contributed to your campaign was so you could straighten this mess out."

"I fully intend to make sure the laws are upheld," Trent said.

"And," Trudy continued, "I think I made it pretty clear at the time why I contributed to your campaign. Your job is to make sure our streets and schools are safe for the law abiding citizens and you can do that by filing the appropriate charges. Jessica Coffers should be in jail for what she did."

The deep breathing was not working. "Trudy," I said icily, "do you know Jessica Coffers personally? Have you ever had a conversation with her?"

"Gillian," Trent said, smiling through clenched teeth.

Trudy set her purse on the desk. "I'm glad to say I don't know her, nor have I spoken to that evil girl."

"If you knew her personally," I said evenly, "you might change your mind about her being an evil girl."

"Nonsense," Trudy sat in the chair I had vacated. "I didn't have to personally know Ted Bundy to understand that he was an evil man." She turned her head to address Trent. "I came to have a conversation with you." She cocked her head in my direction. "How long is she going to be here?"

I inhaled deeply.

"She was just leaving," Trent came around the desk and took my elbow. He escorted me out to the reception area. "Don't," he said in a low voice, "antagonize my constituents."

"Why not? You do." I whispered back.

He let go of my elbow.

"You have the paper with the names?" I asked.

"In my pocket," he answered.

"And you're going to make that a priority?" I asked.

He patted the shirt pocket. "My top priority," Trent said.

"Call me if you find something," I said.

"Count on it," Trent said. He turned, walked back into his office and closed the door.

SIX

Russ Johanson's office was across the street from the courthouse. It was the noon hour and I hoped Russ was in his office. A bell jingled as I opened the door and walked into the reception area. To my left was a desk with two chairs in front of it and to my right was an uncomfortable looking bench and a coffee table. Other than three magazines and an arrangement of plastic flowers, the room was bereft of any decor.

Russ came into the reception area. "Gillian, what can I do for you today?"

"I wanted to talk to you, if you had a few minutes," I said.

Russ's forehead furrowed in concentration. "Of course. Now if I remember right, you and Clint combined your home owners and auto last year."

"I didn't come to talk about insurance," I said. "I'm here because of a conversation I had with your dad."

"Dad?" Russ was genuinely surprised.

"We were talking about your sister, JoJo."

Russ's mouth fell open for a second and he looked out the window and into the street before looking back to me. "Why don't you come back to my office?"

I followed Russ down the short hallway and into his office. The office was about half the size of the reception area and, unlike that space, had papers covering every available surface. A credenza to the side held a perking coffee maker and a half-eaten sandwich along with photographs. Some of the pictures had been knocked over to make room for a stack of thick folders and I recognized some of the names on the tabs as people I knew in Bend Brook. The wall above held diplomas and certificates and a cloth banner that proclaimed Russell Johanson as the 1998 Underwriter Of The Year. The chairs around the desk all held papers and files. Russ moved a stack of three-ring binders from one of the chairs. "Have a seat. I was just checking rates on car insurance. Companies are so competitive nowadays."

"Should I refer to your sister as JoJo or Rebecca?" I asked.

"She'll always be JoJo to me," Russ sighed. "I suppose this is about the call she got on Christmas?"

"No," I said, surprised at the question. "I don't know anything about a call. It's about the man who attempted to rape her when she was in college."

"I see." Russ sighed again. "Sometimes you have to take Dad with a grain of salt."

"Your father thinks he was someone from Bend Brook?" I waited for Russ's reaction, but he started rearranging things on his desk. "Did JoJo ever mention anything to you that would indicate she thought it was someone from Bend Brook?" I persisted.

Russ stopped reorganizing. "Oh, no, JoJo never got a good look at him. He was wearing a mask."

"Did she mention anything else, anything to indicate it was somebody she knew?"

Russ looked to the wall with the certificates and exhaled. "No, but I never personally discussed that aspect with her. Dad was sure it was someone from here and, to be honest with you, sometimes I have thought that, too. Anymore, I just don't know what to think. You probably should know that in some ways Dad took this worse than JoJo. She went on with her life and it has just sort of stuck with Dad."

"She must have taken it badly, though, or she wouldn't have dropped out of college."

Russ dug through the pile of photographs and pulled one out. He looked at it and handed it to me. I recognized Russ as a boy of about eleven or twelve in the framed close-up picture. He was down on one knee, next to a little girl of about three or four. The little girl was wearing overalls and had a baseball cap perched cockeyed on her head, on her hand was a large baseball glove and someone had thrown a ball that would fall directly into it. The little girl's mouth was open in happy amazement and you could see it was Russ's arm guiding her glove so the ball would fall into it. "I love this picture," Russ took it back and looked at it fondly.

"I was the next oldest to JoJo and I think I was the closest to her. Of course, by the time she was in high school, Rob and I were the only brothers she had left in Nebraska and Rob was more like a father figure than a brother. Probably because of the age difference. Anyway, I think I was the only brother that JoJo confided in and she told me she wanted to drop out of college before this ever happened. She just didn't have a reason that Dad would accept."

"Did she have to have a reason?"

Russ smiled. "In our family, yes, she would have had to have a reason."

"Why did she want to drop out?" I asked.

He put the picture on his desk so it faced him. "She wasn't sure what she wanted to do with her life. When she went to college she was going to be a teacher, and then sometime in her freshman year she decided she didn't want to do that. Computers were the big thing back then and she switched to take some computer classes, but she didn't like those at all. JoJo told me she thought she should take a year off until she knew what she wanted to do."

"Did she ever go back to school?"

"Not really. She took some classes now and then," Russ said.

"From what your dad told me, I think he is pretty sure that the reason she didn't finish college is because of the attempted rape. You're sure that didn't have any impact on JoJo dropping out of college? It must have been an unsettling experience for her."

"If it was such an unsettling experience, wouldn't she have moved back home? Or at least out of the apartment she lived in at the time? Well, I guess she did move to Omaha, but that was later." Russ shrugged his shoulders. "She just dropped out of school. I don't know exactly what she said to Dad after this happened, but she had been telling me for months that she didn't want to go to college."

"Russ," I began hesitantly, "do you think maybe she just said a man tried to rape her so she could use that as an acceptable reason to quit school?"

Russ lost his usual air of good humor. "No, JoJo would never do that. If you had known her, you wouldn't even suggest it."

"I didn't know JoJo," I conceded, "and I didn't mean to offend you. It just sounded like she wanted to drop out and was looking for a reason. And you just said it didn't affect her otherwise."

"Don't get me wrong. I talked to her every day for probably a week after it happened, just to make sure she was okay, and she told me she had bought pepper spray and some device that you could press and it would sound like a police siren. She also signed up for a defense class." Russ started stacking files on the side of his desk. "Maybe that's the difference between JoJo and Dad. JoJo did things to deal with it and Dad never did. They just came away with completely different attitudes. In fact, when I asked JoJo if she was doing okay a couple of months after it happened, she said she was fine and had decided to make it a positive experience."

"A positive experience?" I repeated.

"Wait," Russ said fanning a hand at me, "don't take that out of context. JoJo said it made her realize that there were people in the world that would hurt her if they got the chance."

"And she didn't realize that before?"

Russ exhaled. "Let me try to explain it better. The police had left a brochure on a victim's support group and she started going to it. She said she considered herself very lucky that her roommate walked in about two minutes after the guy got there, but even more so after going to this group. She said really awful things had happened to some of the women there and sometimes she felt guilty for even going because nothing truly bad had happened to her. She kept going to that support group and to a self-defense class, though, because she told me if she was ever in a situation like that again she wanted to be tough and able to do something about it rather than just panic."

"I would think she'd be pretty tough, growing up with four older brothers."

Russ picked up the picture. "JoJo was the glue that held our family together, but she wasn't tough."

"How did JoJo hold your family together?" I asked out of curiosity.

Russ put the picture back. "After Mom died, it was hard. People felt sorry for us, especially for JoJo. They doubted whether Dad could raise a baby. Of course, all that speculation about his ability as a parent was just a battle cry to Dad. He said it was his job to see that all of us turned out well, and he would see to it that we did. He made out charts of who would make supper, who would do laundry, and who would watch JoJo. I really can't say that it was ever a burden to any of us. We just all came together to pitch in, especially with JoJo. It's not like we were perfect kids, my brothers and I used to argue and fight, but now that I think back, I can't remember ever fighting with JoJo. She was a great kid and we all just loved her. Rob was sort of bossy with her, but he always had her best interest at heart. Maybe I'm still doing a poor job of explaining this, but that's what she expected of everyone, that same patience and kindness and the world just isn't like that. That's why she thought that guy attacking her had a positive side to it, because it reminded her that you have to watch out for the bad things in the world." Russ turned around to pour some coffee. "Does that make sense to you?"

"I can understand that." I took the cup of coffee Russ offered me and watched while he poured another cup for himself. I took a sip of my coffee. "What I don't understand is why it's so important to your dad to find out who it was. Especially since JoJo has been dead for over ten years."

Russ winced.

"I'm sorry," I said. "I didn't mean to sound callous."

"It's not so much JoJo as Dad right now. You know Dad has cancer?"

"Yes," I nodded.

"Well, of course you do. Everyone that's seen him would know." Russ paused. "Here's another of those concepts that I'm not sure I can explain. Dad knows he won't be with us much longer and I think he is trying to finish everything he started. I think he feels he finished with my brothers and me, but there are loose ends left with JoJo and he wants to take care of those before he goes."

"I could understand that concept better if she were alive," I said hesitantly.

Russ set his coffee cup down and picked up a pen and started doodling on his calendar. "He thinks this rapist is tied to JoJo's death."

"Wait," I said. "Your dad said she died in a car accident and if I understood correctly, that would have been years afterward."

Russ put down the pen and picked up his coffee. "That's correct."

"Was it a suspicious accident?" I asked.

He shrugged. "She lost control of the car. She was alone at the time."

"Russ, that doesn't make sense. Why would your dad think there's a connection?"

"Because of the call on Christmas Day," Russ answered.

"What call on Christmas Day?" I asked.

"He didn't mention that at all?"

"No," I shook my head.

"Well, there was this phone call. Like I said, it's Christmas and we were all at Dad's house. It's a big deal because everyone was home, both of my brothers from out of state and Rob's family and me and my family and JoJo. Rob wanted to have it at his place but Dad insisted we all be at the home place. There were twenty-five or thirty people and everything was just chaos, the kids were playing and screaming and all the women were in the kitchen saying what they should have gotten Dad for Christmas after seeing what he has for cooking utensils. It was just a great Christmas. The phone rang and Dad answered it and said it was a man asking for JoJo." Russ stopped talking and started wiping dust from the side of his computer.

"And that was significant, that she'd get a phone call?"

"Yes, it sort of was because the caller asked for JoJo and she'd been trying to get us all to call her Becky. She could be insistent that we call her Becky and she and Rob got into a big fight about it once. Anyway, she seemed really excited after she got off the phone, and I got the impression that the guy who called her was a big deal. I asked her why she hadn't brought him to our Christmas dinner and she said she hadn't seen him for a while, but she might invite him to the next family celebration. She said they were going to meet for lunch the next day and she just sparkled when she talked about it."

"Who did she meet?"

"That's just it. We don't know. She never said a name." Russ's brow furrowed. "After the accident, though, we found out that she had met a man at a restaurant in Omaha and, according to one of the waiters at the bar, the guy didn't stay too long but she stayed for a couple of hours, just sitting there, finishing her drink."

"So the accident happened the day she met the guy who called her JoJo on the phone?"

Russ nodded.

"Maybe she was waiting for someone else who didn't show." I shrugged. "Or maybe she just wanted to finish her drink."

"That's the other odd thing. JoJo didn't drink."

"How can you be so sure?" I asked. "Maybe the meeting was supposed to be some sort of celebration."

"I don't think so. At Christmas dinner we had wine and she wouldn't have any. Not even for a toast. She said drinking was unhealthy and she had just started taking some prescription medication that shouldn't be taken with alcohol."

"That is odd. But I'm still confused as to why you or your dad would think this would tie in to the attempted rape."

Russ gave me a look that was partly apologetic. "Dad thinks that the person who called on Christmas was the same person who tried to rape her, only this time JoJo realized who it was and it upset her enough to make her combine alcohol and prescription medicine and have an accident. So you see Gillian, Dad has, or thinks he has, an axe to finish grinding over this."

I sipped my coffee. "Do you think there is a connection?"

"Well," Russ colored slightly, "at times I have. Who would know to call her at Dad's on Christmas Day and ask for JoJo? It must have been someone from Bend Brook."

"I wonder why your dad didn't tell me this."

Russ picked up a pen and started clicking the top. He gave me a baleful smile. "Don't be offended, but he probably wanted to see if you could find it out on your own. It's his way of testing people."

I pulled a paper and pen out of my purse. "One last thing. Do you remember the name of JoJo's roommate? The one who stopped the attack?"

"Of course I do. Her name is Lark. Lark McCallister."

"Lark McCallister," I repeated. "I wonder if she's still in the Lincoln area."

"Are you thinking about contacting her?" Russ asked.

"Possibly. If I can find her. She might have married or moved away."

"No, she lives in Omaha. You won't find her in the phone book, but I have her address and number."

"You've kept in touch with her?"

"I handle her insurance. And we talk occasionally. We both like to play the stock market and at one time we'd had our money invested in some of the same stocks."

"I had quite a different impression of her from your dad. He didn't seem to like her."

Russ smiled. "Your impression is correct. Dad has never liked her. He thought Lark was a bad influence on JoJo."

"But you don't think so?"

"I wouldn't say she was a bad influence. I don't think she leads a conventional life but that doesn't necessarily equate to bad. She's just very different from JoJo."

"Maybe that's why JoJo liked her," I said.

"Yes, that could be it. Like the old saying, 'opposites attract.' I never would have expected JoJo or Lark to be roommates, but they seemed to hit it off when they lived in the dorm."

"Ahhh," I said. "They were roommates by chance."

"At first, yes. But they moved off campus after their freshman year and at that point they were roommates by choice. It must have worked out pretty well because they were still roommates when JoJo had her accident."

"Really? Could I have Lark's address and phone number?"

Russ fidgeted. "As her insurance agent, I can't give it out. As her friend, I'd like to get a hold of her first." He paused. "You really think you need to talk to her?"

"Lark was the one person who was an eyewitness," I reminded him. "It would help me if I could ask her some questions."

"Let me call her. She might be," Russ paused, "more cooperative if I give her a heads up."

SEVEN

The next person on my list was Rob Johanson. Rob's house was not visible from the road, but the mailbox and a large green sign at the end of the driveway identified the residents who lived there as well as the seed corn they endorsed. A feedlot ran alongside the drive on the right, on the other side of the drive was an empty pasture. Past the feedlot, the driveway curved to the left and revealed a large square farmhouse with a wraparound porch. Pots of red geraniums and a wicker love seat were on either side of the front door. A cat curled on the loveseat paid no attention to my arrival, or to the large, shaggy dog noisily announcing my presence.

A girl of about ten or eleven came to the doorway. She had brown hair and blue eyes and a sturdy build. "Sadie, come here!" she spoke sharply to the dog.

I rolled down the window. "Is your dad home?"

"Nope. He's in the field. Mom will be home from work in about an hour."

"It's your dad I wanted to talk to. How soon will he be back?"

"He'll probably keep at it for another couple of hours. Then he'll come in and sleep for a while before he goes to his other job."

"Do you suppose I could go out to the field and talk to him?"

She wrinkled her nose and thought about the question. "I don't know. I'll call him. He's got a cell phone with him." The girl came down the porch steps, took Sadie by the collar and drug her back. "You can get out, she won't hurt you."

She let go of Sadie after I was out of the car and I muscled past the dog to follow her into the house where she had already started dialing on the kitchen phone. "Gillian Jones wants to talk to you." I hadn't told her my name. It reminded me of the old TV show with "just the facts, ma'am." She listened, said okay and hung up. "I'll go out with you. He's heading towards the road and he'll stop to have a sandwich and talk with you for one minute." Her emphasis was on the word "one," and I knew a minute was all I'd get.

I watched as she pulled a small wicker picnic hamper out of a cupboard and then buttered four slices of bread. Next she took a summer sausage out of the refrigerator and sliced several pieces. I admired how evenly she sliced. It wasn't one of my strong points. She carefully wrapped some cookies in a napkin and poured a thermos of coffee, filled another thermos with ice and water, and then put everything in the hamper. "Okay, let's go."

She directed me to a road that bordered the side of the empty pasture and pointed to a tractor in a field. I pulled the car into the shallow ditch and we got out. Rob reached the end of the row and turned the tractor around to start the next one. He cut the engine and climbed down from the tractor cab. Robert Johnson, Jr. couldn't have been more than twenty years younger than his father and, like his father, he was tall and thin with hair that had gone mostly to gray. Something in the way he moved told me he was not in a good mood.

The girl took the sandwiches out of the hamper along with the cookies and the thermos of coffee and water. Rob poured a cup of water and drank from it, then sat down on the back of the tractor. The girl handed him the sandwiches and cookies.

"I'll pass on the cookies," he said.

"Do you want one?" she asked me. "I made them myself."

They were chocolate chip cookies, round and golden and delicious-looking. "Thank you," I said, taking one. I bit into it and jarred my teeth on the unyielding cookie.

"They've got too much baking powder," she explained. "I used tablespoons instead of teaspoons. But everyone says they're the best looking cookies they've ever seen."

"They do look nice," I said.

"Leave the cookies," Rob said to the girl. "Take the basket and go back home."

"But she said she would give me a ride," the girl responded.

"I said go home. Now scoot."

Her lips narrowed slightly, but she nodded once, grabbed the basket and went across the road and under the fence into the pasture.

Rob threw the rest of the water out of the cup and poured coffee into it. "Here," he said offering it to me. "It helps if you dunk them."

"Thanks." I put the cookie in the coffee and watched it disintegrate.

Rob poured himself coffee from the thermos and unwrapped one of the sandwiches without saying another word.

"I'm sure you wonder why I wanted to talk to you," I said.

He stopped chewing. "I know why you came."

"You've talked to Russ?" It had been less then an hour since I'd left Russ's office.

"No. I talked to Dad yesterday. He told me he was going to hire you." Rob looked at me directly, and I saw his blue eyes were hard and angry. "Just how much are you charging him for this?"

The question caught me by surprise. "Nothing. He offered to pay and I told him I couldn't take any money."

Rob took off his seed cap and wiped the sweat from his brow with the back of his hand. "Then why are you doing this? JoJo's been dead for over ten years."

"Look," I said, "I tried to tell your dad no to the whole thing, but he's, you know, sick."

Rob took another bite and looked off into the distance. He swallowed and looked back at me with a rueful smile. "He's a hard man to say no to, even when he's not sick. He's always lived on his own terms and now he's bound and determined to die that way, too. You know he quit his chemotherapy?"

"No, I didn't know. Is his cancer treatable?"

"Treatable to the extent that the chemo would keep the cancer from spreading, but it wouldn't cure him. Only thing is, the chemo makes him real sick and he either has to go to the hospital or have someone come in and take care of him. He told the doctor that wasn't how he was going to live and he'd just die when he was supposed to die."

"That must have been a hard decision for him," I said.

Rob nodded. "He can be a hard man." Rob took another drink of coffee and looked me in the eye again. "Except when it came to JoJo. He was soft as warm butter with her and she just ran through him every chance she got."

"JoJo?" I asked, unable to keep the surprise from my voice. "I heard she was a really good kid."

"I always used to think that, too," he said.

"And now you don't?" I asked, my interest piqued.

He looked into the distance again. "She was spoiled. She got away with stuff she shouldn't have."

"Like what?"

"Well, like insisting we call her Becky. She told us she was going to go by Becky at college. Okay, fine, no problem there. Then, I think it was the next Easter she tells us all that her name is Becky and she's not going to answer to JoJo. And she wouldn't! If we didn't call her Becky, she ignored us. Hell, I've called her JoJo since the day she was born and I told her 'we're your family, you know we mean you if we say Becky or JoJo.' Next thing I know my Dad's telling me if she wants to be called Becky, we will call her Becky. I don't think any of us boys would have gotten away with that."

"Her name would have been important to her, though."

"Oh, it wasn't just the name. Every time I talked to her after she went to college, she had a different major. My oldest is in college and I've got a son heading there this fall. I've told them both they'll only get one chance at it on my dime. And that's how it was for me and my brothers, too. But not for JoJo. After she dropped out, she'd talk about going back to school and sometimes she'd sign up for classes. Dad always supported her but then she'd just fiddle faddle around. If my kids pulled that crap or partied the way JoJo did, I'd be hauling their asses home so they could work a couple of jobs and pay their own way through school."

"Wait," I said, shaking my head, "just because JoJo couldn't decide what she wanted to do doesn't necessarily mean she was out partying."

"Oh, yeah? A couple of years before her accident, I called her at eleven o'clock on a weeknight and I told that poor excuse for a woman that she lived with for JoJo to give me a call. I don't hear from her, so I think she didn't get the message. I call again at seven the next morning and her roommate tells me she came and left. That was just bullshit; she was lying through her teeth. So I started calling late at night and early in the morning and that girl was never home. She'd call me back most times and I never made a ruckus about it, but I wanted to let her know I knew what she was doing."

"You know, I didn't get the impression from Russ or your Dad that she was a partier."

"Well, she never was around here. In fact, a summer or two before she died we were all at my house for the Fourth of July. My wife asks JoJo if she wants a beer, except she has to say Becky so then she'll know that she'll get a response. 'Oh, no,' JoJo says if front of all of us, 'I'm on a high energy diet and alcohol is just empty calories.' I could of given her a prescription for more energy: Go to bed at night and quit drinking." Rob tore another bite out of the sandwich.

I shrugged. "Just because she was out at night doesn't necessarily mean she was drinking."

Rob stopped in mid chew and looked at me in surprise. He swallowed and said "Didn't Dad tell you about her accident?"

"He said she died in a car accident." I said. "Russ told me she'd met someone for lunch and had a drink when she was taking medication that shouldn't be combined with alcohol."

"Did either of them tell you her blood alcohol level was .13? She was over the legal limit and it wasn't even four o'clock in the afternoon," he said in disgust.

I felt defensive for JoJo. Or maybe for Russ. "But the waiter said she sat there alone for a while. And Russ told me something might have upset her."

Rob finished the last of the sandwich before answering me. "Dad and Russ have blinders on when it comes to JoJo. Dad wanted her life to turn out different, but what's done is done. He can't change anything now, neither can I, and neither can you. So if you'll excuse me, I've got to get back to work." I dumped my coffee and handed Rob the cup. He gathered up the wrappers and the thermoses and climbed back into the tractor cab. I threw the remainder of my cookie in the ditch on my way back to the car.

EIGHT

After I left Rob, I called Clint from my cell phone to let him know I'd be home soon.

"Gillian, do you have any lettuce?" he asked

"I don't usually carry lettuce with me," I answered.

"No," he said. "I meant at your office. Georgia Lohrmeister told Mom she was dropping off a box of garden produce this afternoon, just for you. She said there was some lettuce in there."

Georgia was my mother-in-law's best friend and she probably thought she was doing me a favor. I really needed to have that little chat with Dot.

"Gillian? Are you there?" Clint asked.

"Yes, I'm here," I replied, gritting my teeth as I drove across a portion of the gravel road that was the equivalent of an antique washboard.

"What's the matter?" Clint asked.

"Nothing that can't be fixed with a stop at the produce section of the local probation office and few words with Dot," I said.

"Oh," Clint said. "You know, the lettuce isn't that big of a deal," he added.

"I'll stop," I said as I turned onto the highway. "I'll be going right by the courthouse."

"I'll see you soon, then," he said.

I pulled in front of the courthouse and had an imaginary conversation with Dot on the way to my office. No real conversation was going to materialize since it was now a few minutes after five and it appeared that everyone had left the courthouse. I unlocked the main door to the county offices on the second floor and walked through the public waiting area to my office. I unlocked my office door. There was the usual faint smell of Pine-sol, but there was a faint musky odor, too.

I went over to the box on the produce table. There was a note on the box: *If there's any lettuce left, it should probably be kept in the fridge overnight. Also, the onions and scallions need a cool, dry place. P.S. The bag on the desk is for Gillian, please don't take it.*

Great, I thought as I went over to inspect what had been left on my desk. It was lettuce, very nice Bibb lettuce. As I put the other lettuce in the refrigerator, I noticed the red light on my office phone was blinking madly. I picked up the phone and pressed the access button. "You have six messages, first message," the prim automated voice announced. "Gillian," the message began, "this is Trent. You've probably left for the day." A pause. "Never mind. I'll try you at home."

I pressed to hear the next message.

"Trent again. Call me as soon as you can."

I pressed again. "I'd like to meet with you," the voice was soft, but had an undertone of urgency. "Soon. Please call me and let me know when you can see me." There was no name or number left with that message but I knew the soft, Southern drawl of Jessica Coffers.

I pressed again. "Gillian, where are you? And why don't you have your cell phone number on file at the office?" Trent sounded irritated. "I've got something that you really need to see. Call me ASAP."

The next message was from Jessica. "I'll come by at 10:30 tomorrow morning. Call me if this is not okay."

The last message came at 3:42 pm. "Gillian, this is Trent. Again! I've got to go take care of some yard work at my house. I'm bringing my briefcase home with me because I've got a copy of a report that I want to discuss with you. It's, well, it's something that you will find very interesting. I also have some questions for you. Call me at home." He rattled off his cell phone number and I played that message again so I could write it down.

My heart beat faster. Trent had found something for Bob Johanson. I grabbed my sack of lettuce and hurried out, locking the doors behind me. I hurried down the steps to the first floor and collided with Pastor Jim.

"Whoa, young lady," he said.

The judge was a step behind Pastor Jim. "Gillian, you're certainly working late."

"No, I just stopped to pick up some lettuce," I lifted the plastic bag ever so slightly.

"It's good I ran into you," Pastor Jim chuckled at his joke. "I wanted to talk to you about Bob Johanson."

The judge suddenly pointed to the entrance of the courthouse. "There's someone looking through the glass," he said.

I looked over to the door. "I don't see anyone," I said.

"He was there a second ago," the judge said.

Pastor Jim and I followed the judge outside and saw a man walking away from us. "Oh, it's Scott," Pastor Jim said. He put his hands around his mouth, "Scott! Come back." The man turned, waved and began to walk back toward us. "Scott and I were supposed to meet at Gap's at five. We have," Pastor looked at me, "personnel issues with the musical that need to be discussed."

Scott joined our group. He was a slim man, with white, wavy hair and an even tan. His blue eyes darted from person to person.

"I don't believe you've met Gillian Jones," Pastor Jim said. "She's the probation officer in Jackson County." He lowered his voice slightly. "She's also Ashley's aunt."

"We shook hands.

"I didn't want to interrupt you," Scott said to Pastor Jim.

"Oh, we were done," Pastor Jim said, "but then I saw Gillian and I just wanted to tell her to disregard a request that Bob Johanson had made."

"Disregard?" I said.

"I told Pastor Jim about Bob's request of you regarding JoJo," the judge said.

"I'll speak to Bob," Pastor Jim said. "I think I'd better clear some time to see him this week. He needs to find some peace before he dies, and he won't find it while he's on some wild goose chase."

"No," I said.

"No?" the judge questioned.

"He might be on to something," I said.

Pastor Jim shook his head. "That's doubtful."

"Maybe not," I replied

"Yesterday you considered it a lost cause," the judge said. "Have you changed your mind?"

"I asked a few people about it, like we discussed," I said to the judge, "and I think Bob might be right. It might have been someone from Bend Brook. I also found that there were similar instances," I glanced at Pastor Jim and Scott who were both watching me intently, "involving girls from Bend Brook who were close to the same age as JoJo."

The judge's forehead furrowed and his eyebrows came together. "That might be cause for speculation, but informing Bob that there might be similar cases wouldn't give him peace of mind."

"Perhaps I should see Bob this evening," Pastor Jim said. "I thought he had put all this behind him, but it sounds like he's still agonizing over it."

"Okay," I said, "but if you see him, tell him I'll be in contact with him soon."

"Do you really think that's wise? All of us here," Pastor Jim indicated the judge and Scott, "know Bob. We've all tried to help him come to terms with his life. I hope you aren't going to open old wounds."

All three were looking at me like I was guilty of something. "I told him I'd get back to him if I found something, and I'm going to do what he asked."

The judge's eyebrows went up. "Are you saying you found something?"

"I think Trent Green did," I said.

"Why would the county attorney be involved in this?" Pastor Jim asked.

"I asked Trent Green to see if he could get copies of the old police reports," I paused, "and he left me a message saying he has an investigative report that I need to see."

"A report on JoJo?" Scott asked.

"It might not be a report on JoJo," I said. "I asked Trent to see if he could get reports on other girls from Bend Brook. I wanted to see if there were similarities between their attacks and the one made on JoJo. If there were similarities and the rapist was identified, then Bob will probably have his answer regarding JoJo."

"Now, I don't mean to sound defamatory," the judge said, "but Trent does tend to blow things out of proportion."

Pastor Jim's mouth went slack. "I've talked with Georgia Lohrmeister about her daughter for years. Brenda would be about the same age as JoJo."

So much for not giving out names, I thought.

"I'd been aware of those two cases, but I never connected them," the judge said. "Are there more victims?"

"At least one more instance around the same time period," I said.

"That does cast a different light on things, doesn't it?" the judge said.

"Maybe it would be better if we met another time," Scott said, looking at his Rolex.

"Scott, I am sorry," Pastor Jim said. "As you can see, sometimes, it's just one crisis after another." He turned to me. "When are you going to meet with Trent? I need to know what's going on so I can counsel Bob accordingly."

"I'll see him tonight," I said.

"After work hours?" the judge asked.

"Trent left me a message that that he took the report home in his briefcase so, yes, I'll go out there tonight. I want to see what he found."

"Out there?" Scott asked. "Doesn't he live in Bend Brook?"

"No," Pastor Jim said. "He rents a house outside of town. We could go right now, Gillian."

I looked at my watch. "I really have to go home first," I said. "Clint's making supper. I might go later. Besides, I'll have to get directions to his house first."

"I can meet you there later," Pastor Jim said. "The house is easy to find, it's north out of town, the first left turn past the water tower. The house he rents is a straight shot from the highway and Georgia Lohrmeister says the grass is going to be thigh-high by the Fourth of July if he doesn't cut it, so it should be easy to recognize."

"Why don't we meet before practice tomorrow?" Scott said to Pastor Jim.

"I'm sorry, Scott. I can't seem to finish a conversation, can I? And you need to get home to Lillian. Tomorrow at noon would be better, if it's not too much trouble," Pastor Jim said.

"Tomorrow at noon," Scott said and began walking away.

"Is your car at the hall?" Pastor Jim called after him. "I can give you a ride."

"No, it's parked around the corner," he called back over his shoulder.

"Shall we meet at Trent's house?" Pastor Jim asked me.

I didn't want to meet Trent with Pastor Jim along. It was hard to predict what Trent had found or what he would say, and I certainly didn't want Pastor Jim there if Trent was still in deal-making mode. "Right now, I really need to go home," I said. "Clint's waiting for me."

"I really don't see any reason why this can't wait until morning," the judge said. "Trent's generally in his office by eight, if not before."

"That's true," I said. "I could talk to him tomorrow morning."

Pastor Jim hesitated. "Well, I suppose it could wait until tomorrow morning. You'll let me know what you find out about JoJo?"

"Yes," I said.

"That took a while," Clint said as I walked into the kitchen.

"You'll never guess what happened," I said, putting the bag of lettuce in the sink. I spent the next few minutes washing lettuce and updating Clint on the call from Trent.

"Trent's called here, too," Clint said. "He left two messages. He wants you to call him as soon as you can."

We walked into the dining room where paperwork was spread out all over the dining room table. "What's this?" I asked.

"This is the paperwork from Mary Lee. You need to sign all these," Clint said, pointing to a small stack. "Some lady called about doing a home visit and I thought we'd better get everything else in order. The home visit is set for next Wednesday so I scheduled us for the training video on Tuesday afternoon. We'll have to go to Lincoln for the training video."

"This is really moving fast," I said.

"Well, if Jessica decides we can be foster parents, we'll want to be ready," he said.

I looked at the forms on the dining room table; they were filled out neatly in Clint's handwriting and he had already signed his name. "Am I at the right house?"

"What do you mean?" Clint asked.

"It's just that you usually don't voluntarily fill out paperwork and," I paused, "there is something else that's different, too. I just can't put my finger on it."

Clint looked around the room. "You know, you're right. It's quiet, like there's a storm coming."

"There's no dog barking," I said.

Our eyes met. "Coco," we said.

"She was here when I called you a little while ago," Clint said, "but then I got busy doing this paperwork."

I followed him outside to the fenced-in yard. "Coco!" Clint called. He walked along the fence until he got to the dog house. The fence on the other side had a mound of dirt by it.

"She dug under the fence," Clint said.

"I just don't understand it," I said.

"You don't understand how she can dig under a fence?" Clint asked, sounding slightly irritated.

"No, I don't understand Coco," I said. "We say she's still in her puppy stage, but Karl Kittman's dog is the same age and he can leave Lizzie in the back of his pickup while he comes in for his probation appointment."

"Lizzie stays in the back of the truck at The Implement, too," Clint said, bewilderment in his voice. "And it's useless to try and teach Coco to be a hunting dog, she's scared to death of loud noises."

"Do you think it might be us?" I asked.

"No," Clint shook his head. "I've had other dogs, but they didn't act like Coco. I think it's because she's penned up all day." Clint sighed, "maybe if we spent more time with her."

Somewhere in the distance a dog barked. "Coco!" Clint said. "Get in the pickup. We'll drive along the road until we spot her."

We got in the truck and Clint pulled out on the highway. Our house is the last one on the highway leading out of town. "Should we check and see if the Murphys saw her?" I asked. The house on the other side of the highway was inhabited by a very elderly couple.

"No, they would've called if they'd seen Coco out," Clint said.

The windows were down but the engine was loud. "We won't hear her in the truck," I said.

"I'm going to pull off." Clint pulled onto the shoulder and turned the ignition off. We heard insistent barking coming from the cornfield, but no sign of Coco. We got out of the truck. "Coco!" we both called. Clint slid down the side of the road first and then held a hand out. I took it and followed him into the ditch.

The barking continued but didn't sound any closer. "Maybe she's trapped or stuck in something," he said.

The barking suddenly changed to whining. "She's hurt," I said. "Coco!" I called, while Clint crossed the fence and went into the cornfield.

"There!" Clint pointed to the cornfield where Coco was streaking through a row. He suddenly made a face and in the next breath I knew why.

"Skunk!" we said together.

"Gillian, shut the door to the truck," Clint yelled.

I was closer to the truck but I was wearing sandals and had to grab on to the tall grass to get back up the incline. At the top of the ditch Coco bounded past me and into the open door of the truck. The stench was terrible.

Coco spread herself out on the seat and whined. I covered my hand over my nose and looked over at Clint.

"She's going to have to have a bath," he said.

"Did I mention that I'm supposed to call Trent Green as soon as possible," I said through my fingers.

Clint held part of his shirt sleeve over his nose. "I thought you said that could wait until tomorrow morning," he said.

We both looked into the pickup at the panting dog, who appeared to be trying to wipe the smell off with her paws.

"It's becoming more appealing by the minute," I said.

"Well, hold your nose and get in the truck so we can get back to the house," Clint said.

NINE

After blocking Coco's escape route with some boards and supplying Clint with two large cans of tomato juice along with the garden hose and my eternal gratitude, I sat down on the steps and dialed Trent Green on my cell phone. No answer. I tried again.

"That's odd. He doesn't answer," I told Clint.

"Maybe he's not at home," Clint said, pouring the last of the tomato juice on Coco.

"But it's his cell phone. He'd have it with him," I said.

"Good point. That is sort of strange, isn't it?" Clint said.

"I might drive over there," I said, picking up the empty tomato cans and putting them in the trash barrel. "I'd really like to see what he's got."

I tried Trent's cell on my drive over; I hoped this wasn't some wild goose chase, or worse yet, a far fetched plan to draw attention to Trent. The place Trent rented was about four miles out of town. It was a small frame house, situated close to the road. The house was surrounded by trees and an overgrown lawn. I pulled into the gravel driveway and parked behind Trent's white Acura.

The side of the house not visible from the road had been partially mowed. The lawn mower had been left in the middle of the yard, knee-high grass on one side. I looked at my watch, it was nearly eight o'clock. Trent would only have an hour or so of daylight left to finish.

A narrow sidewalk led to three steps and the front door. I got out of the car, went to the door and knocked. The dirt in a potted geranium by the steps was damp. I knocked again and waited while a small black beetle scurried down the side of the planter. I opened the screen door and pounded on the door. Nothing. I turned the handle. It was unlocked. I cracked the door open. "Trent?" I called.

My eyes scanned a living room full of contradiction. The walls had been painted a light lavender and scalloped lace curtains hung on the windows. The background would have been fitting for knick knack shelves and an overstuffed chair. Instead, the furniture was black leather and the coffee table and book shelves were glass and chrome. "Trent?" I tried one more time. On the coffee table, a glass of amber colored liquid — presumably tea — sweated with condensation from ice that had melted away. Trent had to be around here somewhere.

I pulled the door shut and looked around. He would have heard my car pull up. I took out my cell phone and tried Trent's number again. A musical tone sounded from the side of the house where the lawn mower had been parked. I walked toward the sound and caught sight of something in the deep grass to the side of the mower. A shoe. No, it was more than a shoe. It was Trent.

I closed my cell phone and hurried over to him. He was face down and I shooed away several flies that buzzed about his head. A thin line of blood drained from his ear and had started to congeal in the grass. *Start CPR*, a voice in my head screamed. I took hold of his shoulder and hip and rolled him over. Trent's eyes were open and opaque. The screaming voice in my head went silent.

TEN

"And then what happened?" Clint wanted to know the details of the evening. It was after midnight and we were having sandwiches at the dining room table, or at least Clint was having a sandwich. I had lost my appetite.

"After Newt and the rescue unit got there," I said, "a state patrol car pulled up on the road. The next time I looked back at the road, there was a line of patrol cars and a camper they use as a portable evidence room."

"Explain to me again why you couldn't drive your car home?"

"They considered it part of the crime scene. I'll have to wait until the crime scene techs are done, then they'll let me have the car."

"And you don't know what killed him?" Clint asked.

"No, I don't know. He had blood coming from his ear, and . . ." I paused.

"And?" Clint said.

"Well, now that I think about it, the back of his head didn't look right," I pushed my sandwich further away from me.

"We can talk more tomorrow." He paused. "Why don't you go to bed? You look like you need some sleep."

Needing sleep and getting sleep are two different things. My first real sleep occurred after the alarm had gone off. It was nine o'clock when I woke up and saw the note from Clint explaining that he'd called the courthouse and told them I'd be late.

The courthouse seemed unusually quiet when I walked in at a little past ten and went up to the second floor.

Dorcas, one of Dot's two full-time county employees, met me at the glass doorway that opens to the offices on the second floor. "We sent your other appointment home already."

"Thanks," I replied. I had only remembered one appointment.

"But now she's in your office and she won't leave," Dorcas said.

"She?" I questioned.

"Jessica Coffers," Dorcas answered. "Dot unlocked your office because she didn't want her sitting out here all day."

I had completely forgotten Jessica's message that she'd be in at 10:30. I walked past Dorcas and into my office.

A worry line is what my maternal grandmother had called that little crease that some people have between their eyes. Jessica Coffer had such a line and today it was pronounced.

"Hello, Jessica," I said to the small girl who sat slightly hunched in one of the chairs in front of my desk.

"Ma'am," she replied.

"Logan's not with you today?" I asked, as I shut the door.

"No, ma'am."

For the last year, I'd been trying to convince Jessica that she could call me Mrs. Jones and that "ma'am" was not necessary. "You can call me Mrs. Jones, or even Gillian, if you'd prefer," I said softly.

"Yes, ma'am. I . . ." She paused.

"Have Mitch and Kay talked to you?"

She nodded, but didn't look up to meet my eyes.

"Jessica," I said, "your aunt and uncle want what's best for you, and for Logan, too. But my husband and I are not going to start adoption proceedings for Logan without your consent."

She sat up in the chair and looked at me, a new glimmer of interest in her blue-green eyes. "I'd have to say you could adopt him?" she asked.

"Yes."

"You'd just be foster parents?"

"If you wanted us to be foster parents," I said.

She sat up straighter. "Logan said a new word yesterday."

"And what word would that be?" I asked.

"He said 'cucumbers,' only it sounds like tootumbers. He loves them. I made a salad for him yesterday and he ate all the cucumbers out of it and wanted more. I said 'those are cucumbers, do you want more cucumbers?' and he said the word."

"And he isn't even two yet," I said.

"No, ma'am. He'll be two on the tenth of August."

"I don't think many children his age are saying cucumber."

Jessica nodded. "Most kids his age have a vocabulary of about twenty words. Logan is very quick to catch on to things." The worry line came back. "Ma'am?"

"Yes," I said.

"Mitch and Kay are guardians for both me and Logan, since we're both under nineteen. But I'll turn eighteen on the twenty-second of August. Won't I be his mother *and* his guardian when I turn eighteen?"

I sighed. Mary Lee had hit the nail on the head when she said that family law was such muddy water. "I don't know. You'll still be in foster card yourself when you turn eighteen."

"But no one will take Logan away from me?" she asked.

"Clint and I would . . ." I stopped. With Trent gone, there would be no one to file new charges.

"Ma'am?" Jessica asked.

"Clint and I would only consider adopting Logan if you thought it would be in his best interest," I said.

"But nobody is going to take him away if I want to raise him myself?"

"That's correct."

"Thank you, ma'am," she said, then paused. "Do I still need to keep my regular Monday appointment since I came in today?"

"Yes, you do," I replied.

"I'll bring Logan with me," she said.

"That would be nice. I'd like to hear him say cucumber."

"We'll bring his new book, too." A smile spread across her face. "Its got a little mouse on some of the pages, and he'll point to the mouse if you ask him to, but only if he's got a mind to do it."

"He's a very smart little boy," I said.

"Yes, ma'am, he is."

My closed office door made a creaking sound. Jessica turned to look at it, then turned back to me and shrugged. I stood up and walked past Jessica to open the door.

Newt, the sheriff, was on the other side. He gave Jessica a suspicious look and then turned his attention to me.

"Do you have a minute?" he asked.

"As soon as I'm finished talking to Jessica," I said, slightly perturbed that he didn't have the decency to knock.

"I was just leaving, ma'am," she said, any trace of animation gone from her voice.

Newt watched her walk out the door, distrust etched on his face. I walked over to the air conditioner and turned it to high while Newt sat down in front of my desk.

Abner Newton III, "Newt" to everyone in Jackson County, was the elected Sheriff of Jackson County. His father had been the Chief of Police in Bend Brook when the town had the funds and slightly larger population to support a police department. I had never really developed a rapport with Newt, but felt a certain amount of appreciation that he'd come to talk to me about Trent. The appreciation mingled with a certain amount of annoyance that he couldn't wait until my office door had been open.

"What have you found out about Trent?" I asked.

Newt had a trim brown mustache, the same color of brown as the wavy hair on his head. He had perpetually wind burned cheeks and depthless blue eyes. "I didn't come here to report to you," he said.

I had momentarily forgotten about the eternal chip on his shoulder. "I wasn't expecting a report," I said, "I thought you'd come with an update on Trent."

"I came with a warning," he said.

"A warning? What are you talking about?" I asked.

"If she," and his head nodded toward the door, "gives even one little piece of incriminating information, you are obliged under the law as her probation officer to report it immediately."

"She came here to talk to me about Logan, she never mentioned Trent."

Newt's eyes washed over me. "That says a lot right there. Most people are itching at the trigger wanting to know what happened to Trent."

"I'm not sure if she's even aware that Trent is . . . gone." Somehow I couldn't bring myself to describe Trent as dead. "Besides, he had," I winced, "blood draining from his ear. It might have been an aneurysm or something. Don't you need to wait for the autopsy before you know for sure what Trent died from?" I asked.

"The medical examiner said he died from blunt head trauma which caused inter-cranial bleeding. They're doing an autopsy today and that's what they are expecting to find."

"And you suspect Jessica did this?" I asked.

"I do," Newt said.

"Trent is," I paused, "or was, six feet tall? Maybe 180 pounds? Jessica is five feet tall, maybe 100 pounds?"

"It looks like someone walloped him from behind," Newt continued. "That wouldn't take hand-to-hand combat."

"And that makes Jessica Coffers your number one suspect?"

"That and an eyewitness who saw the Banner's Taurus speeding away from the scene at about six o'clock."

"Who was driving?" I asked.

Newt shifted. "They couldn't tell because it was kicking up a cloud of dust, but they're ready and willing to sign a sworn statement that it was Kay Banner's black Taurus, which is the car they let Jessica drive." Newt pointed a finger at me. "So if she says something . . ."

"For your information," I interrupted him, "Jessica was here this morning because she was worried about having to give her son up, if she knew Trent was gone, she wouldn't have been worried about it."

"All I'm saying is, I don't want you protecting your little friend if she opens her mouth to you."

Anger washed over me in a tide. "You forget Trent wasn't the most popular person in this county, either," I said. "When I went to his office earlier this week, there was a man from Jacksonville threatening him."

"I've already talked to Doris," he said. "I know all about who was at his office the past couple of weeks, including the person who just paid you a visit."

"Jessica?" I said.

"Yesterday afternoon," Newt said.

I shrugged. "I was at his office yesterday, too. That shouldn't make either of us a suspect."

"The difference is Jessica Coffers had motive and opportunity."

"Someone else apparently had a motive and opportunity, too," I said. "I've already told this to the investigator from the State Patrol last night, but I was at his house last night because Trent had found some police reports that he wanted me to see."

"Yeah, I heard about that," Newt said. "Ain't it funny, though, that you're the only one that seems to know about those police reports?"

I didn't answer. I picked up my phone and punched the numbers to get to my archived messages and played each one from Trent. Newt's face went slightly pale when we heard Trent's voice berate me for not having my cell phone number on file and then state he had a report that I needed to see.

"I'm subpoenaing those phone messages," Newt said.

"The State Patrol already has them," I replied. I had given the information to the investigator who said my messages from Trent would be copied.

Newt got up and I followed him out to the public waiting area. "Wait," I said. "If you want to get to the bottom of this, I'm not the only one who knew about those reports and I may not be the only one who Bob Johanson talked to about his daughter. You should see who Bob . . ."

He swung around and pointed a finger at me, "Don't tell me how to do my job. You just need to remember if she says anything incriminating you are obliged under law to report it." And with that he pushed his way through the glass doors.

I ignored the questioning looks of Judy and the two people in the public waiting area. I went back in my office and dialed the number for Trent's office. Doris answered in a somewhat shaky voice.

"I'm sorry about Trent," I said.

"So am I," she sniffed. "He wasn't Wendell Krackenberg, that's for sure, and he had his faults, but he didn't deserve this."

"I know this is hard for you right now," I said, "but yesterday Trent was going to contact somebody in Lincoln for me. Do you know if he did?"

"You mean about those police reports?" Doris asked.

"Yes!" I nearly screamed.

"I don't know, Gillian. I left right after you got here yesterday, remember?"

"But you knew he was looking for police reports," I said, still hopeful.

"Only because an investigator from the State Patrol asked me the very same question this morning and I didn't know what he was talking about. But then the judge came in and he explained everything to that investigator. They were going up to your office after they left here. It wasn't even eight yet and I said I didn't know if you'd be there."

"They were going to get messages off my phone," I said. "I gave them the access numbers last night when they were questioning me."

"Because you found him," Doris said with a bit of awe in her voice. "Gillian?" she said hesitantly.

"Yes?" I cringed, hoping she wouldn't ask me to describe Trent.

"Something must have happened yesterday afternoon after I left. He had no appointments scheduled and he told me he was going to go over some land surveys."

"Trudy March was in his office when I left there yesterday," I said.

"That's not unusual. She comes in to see him quite a bit about Jessica Coffers," Doris said.

"It's those police reports I asked him to find." I sighed. "He was going to call someone in Lincoln. I though maybe you would know who he would've contacted."

"You know, I think he was good friends with someone in the Lincoln Police Department, but I don't think he ever mentioned a name."

"That's right," I said. "He said something about the records department at LPD and a friend who would help him. Doris, can you tell if Trent had any faxes yesterday afternoon?"

"No, they asked me that this morning, too. They'll have to get phone records."

"Thanks, Doris. That was helpful," I said.

"That's what the investigators from the State Patrol said, too," she replied.

My next call was to my mother-in-law. My car was still behind crime scene tape and rather than take Clint's pickup, I'd borrow Marlene's sedan for a trip to the Records Section of the Lincoln Police Department.

ELEVEN

The only familiarity the Lincoln Police Department had with the name Trent Green was due to the news reports of his death. My failure to leave the premises and my insistence at locating police reports on sexual assaults from the '80s had eventually landed me in the office of an LPD Sergeant. He said there was one person who might be able to help me.

Now I stood on Vine Street in Lincoln, Nebraska. Looking to the west, I saw the football stadium. Clouds hung low in the sky and it reminded me of a temple. On game days, the air vibrated with the sound of band instruments and the sidewalk was jammed with people. Today, in the heat and humidity of late June, the only sounds to be heard were the distant buzz of a lawnmower and the thumping bass from a car driving down Vine Street.

Sidney Weissman lived just off of Vine in a well cared for two-story bungalow, between two less than well cared for bungalows. I walked up the steps to the wide porch and rang the bell. I heard a commotion inside the house and a thick-waisted woman in a house dress opened the door. Her dark hair was pulled back in a bun and she held a wooden spoon in one hand. A small child in a t-shirt and diaper peeked out me from behind her dress.

"May I speak to Sidney Weissman?" I asked.

She scowled. "We don't accept solicitors," she said, starting to shut the door.

I put my hand on the outside of the door to keep if from closing. "No, wait, please, I was referred by Sgt. Kozad."

The door opened. "Humph." The woman looked me over. "Come in, then, before you let all the cool air out. Sid's in his den. Let me see if he's decent." I followed her and the toddler through the living room. Another child of perhaps four sat in front of the television. She stopped in the doorway that separated a dining room from the kitchen. Sliding glass doors off the dining area lead to a sun porch which was littered with children's toys. "Sid," she yelled, "do you have your pants on?"

"Who wants to know?" a man's voice yelled back.

"Ach," she said, "if you find him in his underwear, you find him in his underwear." I followed her into a large, bright kitchen where another child of about seven sat at the kitchen table. Something cooking on the stove scented the air with cinnamon. An added room off the kitchen was apparently the den and Sidney Weissman sat at a card table in an undershirt, sections of the newspaper spread out before him. Suspenders strained against a paunchy stomach and led me to believe he was indeed wearing pants. He looked at me over reading glasses, the top of his head was bald and tufts of graying red hair curled out from the sides. He looked more like an off-duty clown than a retired police officer.

"Sid," she's said. "This woman is here to see you." She turned and left with the child trailing behind her.

"So, you're here to see me?" he said, thin lips carefully forming each word.

"I'm Gillian Jones. I'm a probation officer from Jackson County." I offered my hand. "I was at the Lincoln Police Department trying to find some old reports, and Sgt. Kozad referred me to you."

"He did, did he? Well, sit down." He gathered the paper together and put it on a recliner that was behind him. A tall metal file cabinet occupied a corner. "Do you drink coffee?"

"No, I'm fine, thank you."

"But you do drink coffee?" he asked.

"Yes."

"Delores," he yelled. "She'd like some coffee. Bring the pot."

"No, really, I'm fine," I said.

Gray eyes with spots of blue looked at me over the top of his glasses. "In case you don't know," he said, "I am not fine. I'd like some coffee and the only way I can have another cup is if you have one."

The woman came back, gave me a suspicious look, and set a mug of coffee down in front of me along with a white insulated decanter. "You know you can only have one cup of coffee," she admonished Sid before she walked out.

"I am on a restricted diet," Sid said to me. "Have been for two years. Do you think I look better?"

"I don't know what you looked like before," I said.

"I look the same. Can't say I feel any better either. Still have the same aches and pains. Do you take cream?"

"No, just black."

"Delores," he yelled "she'd like some cream."

"But I don't take cream," I said.

"You came here to pick my brain over something, didn't you?"

"Well, yes."

"So I'm doing you a favor, right?" he asked.

"Yes," I said.

"Then you do me a favor, and take the cream."

"Okay," I said.

Delores came back in, gave me a withering look, and set a cream pitcher and spoon on the corner of the table.

"Shut the door on your way out, we got some confidential business to discuss."

I heard the door behind me slam more than shut.

"Weeee," Sid said, reaching around him to the file cabinet and taking a cup out of one of the drawers. He poured a big dollop of cream in his cup and then poured coffee from the decanter. "Here," he said handing me the cream pitcher.

I shook my head. "No, thank you. I don't take cream."

Sid gazed at me, thin lips forming the words carefully. "But my wife thinks you do. And after you leave, she's gonna pick up your cup and she's gonna look in it and see you didn't use any cream. And then she'll give me holy hell."

I poured cream in my coffee and Sid handed me the spoon. "I hadn't thought of that," I said.

"Then I'll excuse you this one time," he said, taking a sip of coffee. "But you better start paying attention. What are you again?"

"A probation officer."

"Well, you need to pay attention to the details. That's what I used to tell officers when I trained them. Details, details, details. I should still be down there saying it. People need to hear it."

"Did you retire because of your health, then?"

"No, I retired because I'd done my time and the world was changing way too fast. I'm just an old dog who doesn't want to learn a lot of new tricks."

I wondered why the Sergeant had sent me here.

"What?" Sid said, noticing my stare. "You think I look too young to retire?"

"Actually, I thought it sounded like you still wanted to be working. Do you help with your wife's daycare business?"

"Ha!" Sid let out a roar. "This is no daycare. Those are my grandkids."

"You must have a big family."

"No," Sid said. "I got two kids. A boy and a girl. They graduate high school and neither of them gets married. They graduate college and neither of them gets married. Another decade goes by and there's not a wedding bell in sight. The boy lives out of state and I call him and say, 'What? Do I have to come out there and find a woman for you?' My daughter lives here in town and I say to her 'What's the matter that I got two kids who don't know how to get married?' So then my daughter, she turns thirty-six and she gets married. She has four kids in six years and then she decides she needs to go back to school and get a different degree, so guess who's going to watch the kids?"

"Your wife. And you," I said.

"That's right," he nodded.

"And your son?" I asked. "Did he get married?"

"No. And now when I call him I say, 'you're still not married? Well, that's just fine by me.' But enough about that. What in my brain do I have that you want?"

"I'll try and make this short," I said. "I was asked to look into the attempted rape of a college student in the mid-80's and I found out some other girls from the same town were raped around that same time period. I asked the county attorney to get the police reports. He left me a message on my phone and it sounded like he found something, but then he was murdered."

"This is in Jackson County?"

"Yes," I said.

"It was all over the news this morning about your attorney."

"I came to Lincoln to see if I could get those reports myself, or find out who the county attorney had contacted, and Sgt. Kozad sent me to you."

"Ahhhhh," Sid's eyes narrowed. "Tell me what towns are in Jackson County?"

"Bend Brook," I said.

He shook his head. "Not the town or county I wanted to hear," he said. "I had your same idea, you know, about girls being raped all coming from the same town, except the dates are a little off and the town I wanted to hear was Nebraska City. Although what you tell me is very, very interesting. How did you come up with your theory?"

"It started with a man who thinks someone from Bend Brook attempted to rape his daughter." I shrugged. "It just went from there."

"You just moved up a notch in my book for trying to put two and two together." He took a sip of coffee. "Where exactly is Bend Brook?"

"It's between Beatrice and Fairbury, not far from the Kansas border," I said.

"Okay, I know the general area, but I'm not all that familiar with the little towns around here. I'm from the Big Apple, except it wasn't that big of an apple when I lived there."

"What made you want to move to Nebraska?"

"Nothing. I never wanted to move to Nebraska. I wanted to move to California. All the time I'm growing up, people talk about California. The great opportunities, the beautiful weather, the pretty girls, you know, the easy life. So I saved my money and when I'm old enough, I tell my folks, this is it, I'm off to California. But then I didn't get farther than Nebraska."

"You liked Nebraska better?" I asked.

"I couldn't tell you. I never made it to California. I was taking my sweet time seeing the world and by the time I get to Nebraska, I'm low on money so I figure I'll work for awhile before I move on. And then I saw an ad in the paper where they were looking for trainees for police officers. And I had worked for NYPD."

"The New York Police Department?" I said, impressed.

He nodded. "In the stable, cleaning up after the horses. So I got on in the park patrol."

"I didn't know they had horses in the Lincoln Police Department," I said.

"They didn't have horses, just parks. But I took the job thinking it'll just be for a while and then I'll be back on my way to California. Except then it's this and then it's that, and what do you know? I'm still here." He adjusted his glasses and scrutinized me through the lenses. "So tell me more, what similarities did you expect to see when you got these reports?"

"I didn't get the reports! I told you the county attorney was going to get them for me and then he was murdered."

"But you talked to the daughter of the man who reported it to you?"

"No," I said. "She's dead."

Sid slurped his coffee. "A homicide? You should've said something sooner. My guy, the one I'm looking for, he threatened but he didn't kill."

"She wasn't murdered. She died later, in a car accident," I said. "The cases you had? Did you get them because there were similarities?"

"No. I got them because I was the unofficial sexual assault investigator back then. When I started, we didn't have women as police officers. We had matrons and they stayed at the station. Well, when the park patrol ended, I thought I was going to have to do foot patrol but then the chief asked if I'd oversee the cases which dealt with women who had been raped or who'd been in domestic disputes. So that's what I did. And I guess these women just felt comfortable with me because I'm not a super macho kind of guy."

I looked at the straining suspenders and then at Sid's wide face and wire rimmed glasses. "No, I guess not."

He set down the coffee cup. "Okay, that last part was a joke. You need to be a little bit quicker on the take."

"Sorry," I rushed to say. "So, you had the same theory except the town involved was Nebraska City?"

"Yes, there were a significant number of victims that were all from the same town and they were all the same type of girl. The good girl who followed directions. You know? These were the girls who weren't going to mouth back or fight until it was too late and I think our perpetrator knew that, meaning he had to know that about them beforehand. Plus, it was within a six months to two year period after they'd moved away from home." He took a sip of coffee. "How about your victim?"

"I think everything you just said was probably true of her, too," I said.

"Where was she when it happened?" Sid asked. "Was she jogging, going to her car after a night class, what?"

"She was at her apartment and the rapist knocked on her door."

"Okay. Bingo." He pointed a finger at me. "That's a match. He knew where she lived and he showed up there. Did he have a weapon?"

"A knife," I said.

"Okay, now we've got match number two," Sid said. "What did he say to the victim during the attack?"

"I don't know. She wasn't actually raped. Her roommate came home right after the guy got there and he ran."

"So we got ourselves an eyewitness, do we?" Sid's intelligent blue-gray eyes surveyed me. "You know, I always wanted a partner who was a woman. Then I could say things like 'girlfriend, he's going down.' That's what they say on TV all the time. I never got to say anything like that when I was a police officer."

I looked over at Sid's thin lips that had curled into a smile and the tufts of hair sticking out from the side of his head. "Maybe you should go back to work, at least part-time."

"Or maybe some probation officer would want some help."

"You'd help me?" I asked.

"Sure thing, girlfriend." He gulped the rest of the coffee and put the cup back in the file cabinet drawer. "We need to get in touch with the eyewitness, first of all."

"She lives in Omaha. I planned to talk to her," I said.

"Good, you go talk to her. Find out everything you can about the perp. What the guy said, what he wore, if he smelled, if he had an accent, how tall, how heavy, everything."

"Okay," I said.

"Meanwhile, I'll pick the brains of some of my former cohorts and see what I find about Bend Brook. Then I'll go through my files and see what I come up with. I've got a bunch of stuff in there," he pointed to the file cabinet in the corner, "and up here," he pointed to his head. "Then," Sid scribbled something on a piece of paper, "if we think the cases are related, we'll probably have to meet for coffee. And Danish. There's a place in south Lincoln that's got good cheese Danish."

I took the piece of paper Sid offered me. It had a cell phone and home phone along with his name. I wrote my home phone number and cell phone number on one of my business cards and slid it across the table to Sid. "Try the work number mornings," I said, "otherwise my cell phone is the best way to reach me."

"You know," he said thoughtfully, looking at my card and rubbing his chin, "if this is my guy, I'd clear six cases. No charges would come out of it, but hey, six cases is six cases."

"I'll call you after I talk with the roommate," I said, getting out of my chair and going to the door. I opened the door to the kitchen and smelled the cinnamon along with apples. "Whatever you're making smells wonderful," I said to Sid's wife. She grunted a response and made her way past me into the den. I turned to tell them I'd see myself to the door but Sid was looking through a file drawer and his wife was looking in my coffee cup.

TWELVE

I called Russ to get the phone number for JoJo's roommate as soon as I returned to Bend Brook. Russ called back about an hour later. He hadn't just gotten her phone number, he'd arranged everything. I was to meet Lark McCallister at her apartment in Omaha the next day at three o'clock. I had a problem, though. My car still hadn't been released and Clint worked Saturdays.

"You could drop me off at work," Clint said, "and I'd catch a ride home. Then you could take the pickup to Omaha."

I didn't really want to take the pickup to Omaha. "Do you think your mom would mind if I borrowed her car again?"

"I wouldn't think so," Clint said. "Just call and ask her."

"Do you think she'll ask what I'm going to do tomorrow?" I asked.

Clint sighed. "Remember, this is my mother we're talking about."

Several minutes later I was on the phone with Marlene, asking to borrow her car. "Of course you can have the car, Gillian. How about I come over in the morning and we'll go to town together?"

"Actually, I wanted to take the car to Omaha," I said.

"Oh, how nice. It's about time you went to see your mother."

"Mmmm," I said.

"You are going to Omaha to see your mother, aren't you?" Marlene asked.

"No."

Marlene gave a little gasp. "It's the fertility doctor, isn't it? You are going to see the fertility doctor!"

"No, I don't think they are even open on Saturday," I said.

"You know you don't have to tell me why you are going to Omaha," Marlene said primly. "I'll just drop the car off tomorrow morning. I'm sure I'll find a way home."

I looked across the room at Clint who just put his arms up in an I-can't-help-it gesture. I sighed. "Bob Johanson wanted me to check on some things for him and that's why I'm going to Omaha tomorrow."

"That is so nice of you to help Bob in his time of need! I could go with you and help, too."

"I don't think so," I said. "I'm going to see JoJo's roommate."

"Oh," Marlene said. "The one with the colored underwear?"

"That one," I answered.

"Gillian," Marlene shouted into the phone. "I've just thought of something!"

"What is it?" I clutched the arm of the chair. Clint raised his head to look at me.

"I still don't know what I'm going to wear to the church musical and it's less than a week away! I'll have to have something nice since I'm handing out the award, but don't say anything about that, it is supposed to be a complete surprise." She paused. "But you know where I like to shop for clothes in Omaha?"

"Westroads?" I said.

"Westroads!" she repeated. "They've got that shop for plus-size women that I just love. I'm sure I'd be able to find a dress there. What if I went with you and shopped while you," she paused, "dealt with that woman."

"I guess that would be okay," I said.

"Oh, I'm being thoughtless aren't I? Maybe you'd like to shop for something new to wear to the musical, too."

"Um, I'll skip the shopping tomorrow," I said.

"But wouldn't you like something new for the musical?" she persisted.

"I can always shop later," I said.

"Gillian," Marlene said. "The musical is next Friday, a week from today. And don't forget we're having dinner at my house after church on Sunday, so if you want to shop you'd better do it tomorrow."

"I'll just wear something I already have," I said.

"Are you sure?" she asked.

"Yes," I said. "I'll drop you off at Westroads tomorrow and then I'll go see JoJo's roommate."

"Well," Marlene said with resignation, "I hope she's dressed appropriately."

THIRTEEN

Lark McCallister was waiting for me.

She stood in the shaded entrance of her condominium, an arm gracefully draped along the edge of the door as if she were standing next to a person rather than an inanimate object. One of her shapely legs was crossed in front of the other, and her low-cut blue jean shorts exposed a toned stomach and hip bones. She was wearing a sleeveless white midriff shirt that tied below her breasts. The white shirt contrasted with her jet black hair which was cut around her ears and poofed up behind her bangs in a style reminiscent of the 60's. Her mouth turned up at the ends like she was watching something very humorous.

The crow's feet at the corner of the sapphire blue eyes and two lines that creased her neck were the only indications that she was past forty. "Come in, Detective, come in," she moved back and bowed slightly, swinging her arm out to indicate I should go first. I saw from her pose and the fluid movement of her breasts that I needn't have worried about her underwear. She wasn't wearing any.

"I'm not a detective." I walked into a granite floored entry.

A manicured hand swirled in front of my face, "Titles are meaningless, anyway, don't you think? Why don't we go into the living room?" She led the way into a large, airy room with overstuffed furniture. The coffee table and other wood in the room was pine and, although there were no windows, a skylight provided a congenial environment for green plants and a hibiscus tree. Bluesy jazz music filtered softly around the room.

I sat on the couch while Lark settled into one of the arm chairs. I noticed she was still watching me with that bemused expression. "Far be it for me of all people to stereotype, but you just aren't what I expected. But then I didn't expect to spend my day solving crimes, either." She picked up a water bottle, unscrewed the cap and took a sip. "Would you like something to drink?"

"No, thanks," I said. "Russ told you I wanted to ask some questions about JoJo?" I asked. "About the night someone tried to rape her?"

"Ask away." She wriggled her shoulders back into the chair and pulled her legs up underneath her. "Please refer to her as Becky, though. It's what she preferred."

"Of course," I said. "Did you get a look at the man that night?"

"No. He had a pair of panty hose on his head and a red bandana that covered his nose and mouth."

"A bandana?" I asked. "Are we talking about the same thing? Russ said he was wearing a mask."

"I think Becky told her dad he was wearing a mask so Bob would stop asking questions." Lark took another drink of water, still with that same smile on her face. "You came here for the truth, didn't you?"

"Hold it," I said. "Why would she say something that wasn't true, especially to her dad?"

"Becky was just tired of answering their questions. A mask was easier to explain than the panty hose and bandana. She just wanted everyone to drop it. And apparently everyone has, well, almost everyone," she finished with a slight laugh.

"Why do you think this is so funny?" I asked.

"Because it is just so typical of Bob. The Knight in Shining Armor ready to defend his crown and country. If only he had something to defend. And don't look at me like that, if Becky were here she'd agree with me."

"You don't think Becky would want to find out who tried to rape her?" I asked.

Lark shrugged. "It was not that big of a deal. Becky regretted that she had ever mentioned it to her family."

"It wasn't that big of a deal? Russ told me you called the police."

Lark paused and fingered the bottle of water. "Let me tell you about that night and then you'll understand. I came home early, it was a very slow night at work and they let me go early."

"You worked at a bar?"

"Yes, and I'm sure you've heard from the saintly Bob Johanson that it was a topless bar." She paused, waiting for me to respond. I said nothing. "It's good money." She paused again. "Probably more than you make. Maybe you should try it sometime." She took another swig of her water and dared me with her eyes to respond.

"Please go ahead with what happened that night."

Lark gave an exasperated sigh. "Oh, all right. Let's see, I walked into the apartment and it was like coming on stage into a play. Becky was standing there with her mouth open and a hand to her throat. There was a man standing behind her wearing black pants and a light colored shirt. He had a pair of panty hose over his head with the reinforced toe sticking up on top and a red bandana tied over his face. His hand was on Becky's upper arm and I didn't realize it at the time, but he was holding a knife to her back with his other arm. I said 'Hey Becky, who's the rooster?' because that's what he looked like. Becky laughed sort of hysterically and said 'he's a rapist.' I said 'this chicken is supposed to be a rapist?' Then the guy grabbed Becky around the neck and said 'Don't come any closer.' Well, I wasn't going to have some psycho tell me what I could or could not do in my own apartment so I took a step closer. Then Becky started to wrench away and he said 'don't move, JoJo, or I'll kill you.' But he wasn't saying any of this with menace, in fact his voice was changing pitch like he was going through puberty. Becky turned and shoved him away and I yelled 'we've got you now, beak boy' and jumped toward him and he, honest to God, screamed and ran for the door."

"He screamed?"

"He was terrified." Lark's eyes were full of smug satisfaction.

"But you called the police and reported it?"

"Yes. Becky and I talked about it for a little while, and then we decided to call the police. They told us not to answer the door unless we knew who was on the other side, along with other little tidbits of useful knowledge. I think it's the same talk they give everyone. They gave Becky some information on self-defense classes, too. The next day, Becky didn't go to her classes. She had this English instructor she hated and she was flunking a computer class, so she called her dad and said she was dropping out. She sort of blamed it on Chicken Man, which is how we referred to him. Her dad came unglued over it. Bob drove up that day and tried to talk Becky into moving back home and we got into a fight about it. End of story."

"When you say 'we got into a fight,' do you mean you and Becky?" I asked.

"Actually, Bob and I got into a fight because of something I said. Becky was trying to convince her dad that everything was okay and I told Bob I dealt with much worse situations at work. Of course, when my place of employment came up, he got all huffy and judgmental. He said I was to blame for the rapist who had come to our apartment. Bob theorized that since I was a loose and wanton woman, someone had assumed Becky was, too."

"What did Becky say?"

"At that point Becky was just playing peacemaker between us, so I left. Bob did everything he could to try and get Becky to move back to the safety and stagnation of Bend Brook. Fortunately, Becky stood her ground and stayed. So in conclusion, Ms. Private Investigator, or whatever you are, Becky didn't want to go to college and she used the Chicken Man as an excuse to drop out of school. If you want to try to convey that to Bob Johanson, I wish you luck. Personally, I think the best thing you can do is to tell him he needs to let it go."

A door opened and closed somewhere in the condo and I looked to Lark for an explanation of who else was home, but she just smiled and raised her shaped eyebrows at me. An extremely tall woman came into the room. The woman was even more striking than Lark with smooth dark skin that shone like polished mahogany against the white of her pants and tank top. A belt of gold hoops encircled her hips and matching gold rings accented her sandals and purse. Large eyes, almond in shape and color, glanced at me and then were hidden by row after row of tiny braids as she put her purse on the floor. "Sorry to interrupt, I just came in to say goodbye."

Lark smiled in a naughty way. "This is my permanent roommate, LaShawn. She's leaving for a photo shoot in New York."

"Nice to meet you," I said.

"Nice to meet you, too," she answered. "Are you going to walk me to the door?" she said to Lark.

"No, you can tell me goodbye here." Lark set her water bottle down and lifted her arms. LaShawn leaned down into the embrace and they kissed on the lips.

"Call me when you get there," Lark said. LaShawn said she would, gave Lark another kiss, retrieved her purse and walked out. We heard the sound of the garage door opening. "LaShawn's a model and she travels extensively." Lark picked up the water bottle and unscrewed the cap to take another drink. "We're planning to relocate to Canada next year when I retire."

"Aren't you too young to retire?"

"Did I not say I make very good money?" Lark smiled. "I also play the stock market and I play quite well."

"Do you still work at a topless bar?"

"Oh, mon cherie, no, no, no. I work at a private club. I'm what you would call an exotic dancer."

"Is this club for women?" I asked.

"No, the clientele are men."

"But you're gay?"

"Extremely."

A thought occurred to me. "Was Becky a lesbian?"

Lark hesitated for a second. "No."

"But Bob knows you are?"

Lark snorted. "I've never told him and I can't image Becky would have

mentioned it. Believe it or not, Bob did not find much space in his heart for
me and if he had known that his daughter was living with a lesbian, he would
have made Becky's life even more miserable. But speaking of Bob again, are
you going to tell him he needs to give his little vendetta a rest and get on with
his own life?"

"Bob has cancer," I said. "I don't think getting on with life is going to be
much of an option for him."

Lark's eyes widened in surprise. "I didn't know. Russ never said anything.
What kind of cancer?"

"I'm not sure. He's been through chemo and, according to Rob, has
declined to continue." I paused. "He doesn't look well at all."

Lark bit her lower lip in concentration. "Then I take back some," she
glanced at me, "but not all of what I said. Maybe you should tell him you'll
search high and low until you solve this mystery. Then he'll think that someone
has taken the torch from him and after he's gone, you could just drop it."

"I have no intention of dropping it," I said. "At first I thought it was an
exercise in futility, but now I think Bob was onto something. I think it's
someone who knew Becky when she was JoJo."

Lark arched her eyebrows. "I've never said otherwise. In fact, Becky told
the police that night that there was something familiar about him and she
thought she recognized his voice but at the time she just couldn't place it."

"Really?"

Lark nodded. "Really."

"Didn't Becky try to find out who it was?"

"Well, at the time Becky and I just thought it was someone who had
gotten infatuated with her and had tried to take matters into his own hands.
When this happened, Becky was," Lark paused to choose her words, "not
going out with boys. We just thought it was somebody she wouldn't go out
with. Becky said we had deterred someone from a life of crime because we
didn't think he'd ever try anything like that again."

"There were other girls from Bend Brook who were raped around the
same time as Becky," I said. "And they all moved to Lincoln to go to the
University."

Lark slowly unscrewed the cap of her water bottle. "Are you kidding? You
think Chicken Man is a serial rapist?"

"I think so."

Lark shook her head. "No, I think you're wrong. I think it's just
coincidence."

"That's what I thought, too. Then I asked the county attorney to see if
there were any police reports on the other victims. He was murdered the
same day."

Lark's face lost any trace of amusement. "I read about that in the paper." She paused. "The guy who attacked Becky didn't seem capable of murder."

"Bob thinks Becky got a call from the rapist the day before she died. The caller asked for her by the name of JoJo, and she met him the next day for lunch in Omaha. She was alone and drunk when she left the restaurant. Russ considered it unusual for Becky to drink. Russ and Bob both think it might have been the would-be rapist and when she realized his identity, she just couldn't handle it."

Lark stared at the hibiscus tree in the corner. The only sound was the jazz music which now sounded melancholy. "That lunch didn't have anything to do with the Chicken Man," she paused. "You know when you asked me if Becky was gay?"

I nodded."

She really wasn't, but she thought she was for a while. And that was probably my fault."

"Because you tried to change her?"

"No, I didn't try to change her. I only wanted her to broaden her horizons. She was just such a blank slate when we first met."

"I don't understand," I said.

Lark sighed. "When Becky and I were first roommates, we didn't quite hit it off. I thought she was naïve and her goody-goody attitude was just sickening. I used to call her Rebecca from Sunnybrook Farms."

"But you eventually liked her?"

"Yes. I did." Lark looked to the side. "Becky was one of the nicest, most accepting people I have ever met. Back then, I had this huge chip on my shoulder and I used to tell people I was a lesbian just to shock them."

"And you've changed since then?" I asked.

Lark laughed. "I deserved that. But back to Becky, I didn't think I could stand her as a roommate for very long so I told her I was a lesbian expecting her to freak out and insist she be changed to a different room or maybe even to a different dorm but she just said 'Oh. Okay.' And then you know what Becky said to me later? She said 'Lark, how did you know you were a lesbian?' And it was just too much for me. I asked her if she ever look at another girl's butt and she said she had but just to compare it to her own. I'd tell her 'that's one of the signs. You know, you just might be a lesbian' and she'd worry about it."

"That was mean of you."

"Yes, but it broadened Becky's horizons immensely. That's what I mean about her being a blank slate. Back then Becky was just a reflection of what other people wanted her to be. Her dad said she was going to be a teacher so she was going to be a teacher. Her brothers all went to UNL so Becky went to UNL. Becky couldn't even say if she was straight or gay because apparently Bob had failed to tell her and she'd never thought to ask herself how she felt."

"I don't understand what this has to do with the phone call." I said.

"I'm getting to that. Like I said, for a while Becky thought she might be gay."

"Were you and Becky lovers?"

"No. She wasn't my type. But we used to drive to Omaha and hang out at a gay bar together and she met a lot of people there."

"This is after the assault?"

"We hung out there before and after, but this part was after. When Becky quit school, Russ helped her get a job at an insurance company in Omaha. I found a job in Omaha, too, so we moved here. In our spare time, we just ended up hanging out with people who were mostly gay. And she fell in love with this guy named Jonathan."

"Jonathan was gay?"

"He was bisexual. Personally, I think he preferred men, but he was a music teacher at a private school. He could take Becky places and introduce her as his girlfriend and then he didn't have to deal with any of the crap that goes with being gay."

"Becky was happy with this relationship?"

"Becky was head over heels in love. We had a going-in party for her, you know like a coming-out party. And yes, she was happy about Jonathan. She wanted to marry him and the whole works. I think they were together for nearly four years. She moved back in with me, let's see, it would have been the fall of 1992."

"She lived with Jonathan? That's strange. Bob never mentioned him and neither did her brothers."

"Oh, they didn't know and she only lived with him for a year or so, not the whole time they went together. Technically her address and phone number were mine, and I would tell her when she had mail or phone calls. And Jonathan never met Becky's family. Becky asked him to, but I think they both realized he just would not have mixed well with the Johanson family. Eventually, Becky gave him an ultimatum."

"An ultimatum about visiting her family?"

"No, an ultimatum about his life style. Jonathan was bisexual. Becky thought she could change that, but it didn't happen. Jonathan had a succession of boyfriends, and it just drove Becky to distraction. I told her a number of times that there were a lot of other fish in the sea and they didn't all travel in schools but she just kept thinking that some day he'd change. Instead, Jonathan got serious about one of the boyfriends and let the guy move in with them. Becky told Jonathan that he would have to choose between her and the boyfriend and, surprise, surprise, Jonathan picked the boyfriend. Becky was heartbroken and she moved back in with me. Actually, at first she just brought enough clothes for a couple of days because she thought Jonathan would call and want her to come back."

"Did he?"

"Yes and no. He called, but only to bug her about getting the rest of her stuff out so the new boyfriend could redecorate the apartment. And she'd just decorated it the year before. The jerk."

"And this would have been around the time she died?"

"No, it would have been a couple of years before. The year she died, Jonathan showed up at our apartment on Christmas Day. I came back home from my mom's house to find Jonathan sitting by our front door writing a note. He looked wasted and strung out and he shoved the note into his pocket and asked if Becky was home. I told him 'she's not here, she's at her dad's being JoJo.' Which, believe me, Jonathan of all people would have known she'd be with her family on Christmas Day. So Jonathan said, 'do you suppose you could tell her something?' At first I said okay, and then he dropped the bomb."

"What bomb?"

"He was HIV positive. And he had known this for nearly a year but was just now getting around to telling Becky." Lark swung her legs out from under her. "I should have been the one to tell Becky, she probably wouldn't have died when she did, but at the time I was so very angry at him."

"Because he had exposed Becky to AIDS," I said.

"Yes, he should have been more careful. And I was furious that he wanted me to do his dirty work for him. I told him he needed to tell Becky himself. I picked up the phone, dialed Bob's number, and handed it to Jonathan. They decided to meet for lunch the next day."

"And he asked for JoJo when he called?"

"Yes, because he knew that is what her family called her."

"So she met him the next day and ended up getting drunk."

"Wouldn't you? Jonathan basically gave her a death sentence."

"HIV positive doesn't necessarily mean you're going to die immediately," I said.

"Maybe not now, but back then it did. Remember Freddie Mercury from Queen? One day he said he was HIV positive and the next day he was dead. And frankly, I don't know if Becky had an accident or if she intended to drive off the road. She drove straight into a tree, you know. I've never told that to anyone in Becky's family, not even Russ. Who would want to hear that their sister committed suicide?"

Lark looked toward the wall and blinked her eyes. "I felt horrible about

Becky's death. If I had done things a little differently, she might not have died, at least not then. And Bob, in some convoluted thought pattern, blamed me for Becky's death, too. I just went ahead and let him because he had to be angry at someone."

"What happened to Jonathan?" I asked.

"He eventually died of AIDS. I did visit him a couple of times when he was in the hospital. He told me all the people he'd lost which included some of the boyfriends he'd been with during the time he and Becky were together. I told him he really should have a hospital wing named after him."

"And because of that, you were sure Becky had AIDS."

Lark took a drink of water. "There were other signs. She was always tired, she'd had a respiratory infection that she'd been trying to get rid of for months. So now do you understand why she was traumatized enough by the HIV diagnosis to drink herself into oblivion? The Chicken Man had nothing to do with her accident. And really, I don't think he had anything to do with those other rapes. If Becky had thought he was terrorizing other women, she would have gone straight to the police and told them."

"Told them what?"

"She would have told them who it was."

"How would she have know? You said Becky just thought there was something familiar about him," I said.

"She saw him a couple years later and recognized him."

"Where did she see him?"

"In Bend Brook. She'd spent a week with the family and when she came in the door she said 'Guess who I saw?' I told her it was just too impossible to guess who might have been gracing Bend Brook with their presence during her visit. Becky said 'I saw the Chicken Man and you'll never guess where in Bend Brook I saw him.'"

I leaned forward. "Where in Bend Brook did she see him?"

Lark looked at me smugly. "At church."

"I go to the same church," I said. People from church started filing unbidden through my mind. "Did she tell you his name?"

Lark pursed her mouth and screwed up her forehead and for a moment looked closer to her true age. "Not a name I can say right at this moment."

"Did she say anything else about him?"

"She said his wife was with him and she went up to him and said just as sweetly as she could 'It seems to me I've seen you somewhere besides church, but I just can't place where. Can you?' Becky said he absolutely squirmed and she knew she'd hit the nail on the head."

"He has a wife?" I said in disbelief.

"Yes. At least he did then."

"Do you remember anything else that she said?"

"Hmmm." Lark pulled her feet back underneath her. "I remember it was the Fourth of July weekend because Becky said she could have lit some emotional fireworks but she didn't think his wife deserved that, so she didn't say anything."

"Do you think she might have told anyone else who it was?"

"Who would she tell? Certainly not her brothers and definitely not Bob. She might have told Jonathan, they were together back then, but obviously you can't ask him." Lark stopped, took a drink and stared at the hibiscus tree. "Actually, there is one place you might look."

"And that would be?" I asked.

"There's a storage unit in Lincoln. I rented it when we moved to Omaha because I just had way too much stuff. After Becky died, I packed up her personal things and moved them there, too. Bob and the brothers took the rest of her furniture and clothes, but this was her artwork and some poetry. I didn't think her family should have them, but I just couldn't bear to throw them away."

"Did you ever mention these things to Russ?"

"No, I should have. Jonathan had a rug and some other things that should go back to Becky's family, so I put those in that storage unit, too." She paused. "I've been meaning to go through everything and call Russ to pick up the rest, but I've just never gotten around to it."

"Becky's been gone for more than ten years," I said.

Lark shrugged. "Time flies. But if you are looking for a clue to Chicken Man's identity, you might find it there. And while you're there, you could throw away all those old papers. Then I could tell Russ to come and get the furniture."

I wondered if there was any paperwork that was worth going through or if this was just a ruse to get me to clean out a storage unit.

Lark got up. "I'll be right back," she said. She reappeared a minute later with a small silver key. "I'm writing down the address for you," she said.

"It sounds like you want me to clean out a storage unit for you," I said.

"Well, if you'd just throw away the letters and the artwork. There's not that much and I just can't bear to do it. And I do need to get it done before we move to Canada," she added.

"Why are you moving to Canada?" I asked.

"Oh, my dear, everybody is moving to Canada. It's a positive migration. LaShawn and I would be able to get married there – legally."

"Can't you get married in Iowa now?" I asked.

"Well, yes, but they also have national healthcare in Canada. LaShawn and I are in the process of buying a financially challenged art gallery in the Toronto area." She held out the key and the slip of paper to me.

"I thought you said you were going to retire. Why would you buy an art gallery that's struggling?" I asked.

Lark smiled. "Because we could turn it around. We're planning on adding a tattoo and piercing shop. It will make a wonderful new career for me after I retire from my current job." She held out the key and dangled it in front of me. "Please?" she said.

"If there's not that much in the storage unit and you know it's letters and poetry, then there's probably nothing on. . . the Chicken Man," I said.

"But," Lark said, "there's also some other paperwork from her desk. It might be in there."

"I don't want to take your only key," I said.

"It's not my only key. I've got another one."

I folded my arms in front of me. "I think you just want me to clean out your storage unit," I said.

Lark put her head back and laughed.

"What's so funny?" I asked.

"Oh, it's just refreshing to find someone who hardly bats an eye over sexual orientation, but obviously finds cleaning storage units questionable."

I reached out and took the key. "I'll look through it, but I'm not cleaning," I said.

"Oh, please, just throw away the personal things," Lark said. "It would be so much easier for you."

"I'm not making any promises," I said. I stood up and walked toward the front door.

"Wait, I've got a question for you," Lark said.

I stopped and looked back at her.

"If the Chicken Man was a serial rapist, what would happen to him after all this time?"

"As far as the rapes, probably nothing. The statute of limitation is seven years past the date of offense."

"Ahhh," Lark said, "so someone would get off scot-free, so to speak. And wait, wait," Lark moved in front of me and blocked the way to the door. "What about Bob? What are you going to tell him? That Becky had AIDS?"

I looked at Lark. "I don't know what I'm going to tell him yet. I'm not sure that it would give him closure to know about the call on Christmas Day."

Lark leaned against the door frame, arms crossed underneath her breasts. "Then I have another question for you. If you were to find out Chicken Man's identity, would you tell Bob?"

"Yes, I would," I said.

Lark raised her eyebrows. "I know you aren't asking me for advice, but I would think twice about that. If you found out who it was and told Bob, he'd probably round up the boys and they'd go beat the crap out of Chicken Man. Or worse. Then they'd be the ones facing charges. And I can tell you Becky would not want that."

"You're right," I sighed. "It's hard to predict what Bob would do if he had that information."

Lark gave me the sly smile again. "Becky was a generous and forgiving person, but I guess we just can't say the same for the rest of her family." She laughed. "Or her friends."

I put the key and the piece of paper in my purse. I took out a business card, added my cell phone number, and handed it to her. "Here are my phone numbers, in case you think of anything else."

She took the card and read it. "You're a probation officer," she said in a delighted tone. "Just a minute." She went to a phone table in the entryway and opened a small drawer. She scribbled on a piece of note paper and handed it to me. "This is my cell phone. Just in case." Lark opened the door and watched me walk to the street from the shaded porch. "Just imagine," she said, "a couple of hours ago I didn't know what I was going to do with myself this week and now I've got my work cut out for me."

FOURTEEN

Marlene insisted that we stop at my mom's house, even though I tried to talk her out of it.

"We're in Omaha, it would be unforgivable if we didn't stop to say hello to your mother," Marlene said firmly. "And step-father," she added.

"It's already after five o'clock," I said.

"Then they should be home," Marlene replied.

"They won't be expecting me," I said.

"Oh, for goodness sakes, Gillian, they're your parents! I'm sure they'd love to see you."

"They would?" I said doubtfully. My relationship with my mother and step-father had deteriorated since the divorce from my first husband. Before Clint, I was married to Vincent. I had met Vincent at the University of Nebraska at Lincoln where I had a double major in criminal justice and political science. Vincent was in pre-med, and intent on being a doctor. I had wanted an exciting career, maybe with the FBI, but I ended up working for a private investigation agency. Vincent said the only real thing to do with a poli-sci/criminal justice degree was to go on to law school. He thought having a doctor and an attorney in the same household was the perfect plan.

Vincent attended med school in Omaha while I commuted to the law college in Lincoln. A head-on collision on Highway 6 put me in the hospital for six weeks and in a rehabilitation center for six months. The accident wasn't in Vincent's perfect plan and he divorced me, while I was still in the rehabilitation hospital.

I wallowed in self-pity. Not that I didn't have a reason, since my leg had been broken, and my shattered left ankle had to be rebuilt. It took six operations and two years of physical therapy before I was walking normally, albeit without high heels.

Initially, my mother and step-father had mourned the loss of Vincent right along with me and then, while I was still wallowing, they reconciled with Vincent but decided visits with me at the rehabilitation center were "too difficult." Our relationship was distant until I decided to marry Clint. At that point my step-father offered the advice that I should wait for someone who might be closer to the "caliber of Vincent." I, in turn, the child who had always tried to please, offered among other things that he could "shut up." Somewhere in that conversation our distant relationship became a nearly non-existent relationship.

"Have they done something different to their house?" Marlene asked as we pulled into the drive. I surveyed the two-story brick house of David and Elaine Bossart. "They've added a new front door," I said, noting a wood door with opaque glass insets. "The old door was red."

"I think your mother also planted some more flowers," Marlene said, as we walked up the sidewalk. My finger twitched. Should I ring the bell? Should I just casually knock and then walk in if the door was open? I opted for the bell.

"Mmmmph," Marlene made a sound in her throat after I'd rung the bell.

My mother answered the door. "Gillian," she said, more of a question than a welcome. Elaine Bossart was an attractive woman in her early fifties and I was fortunate to have inherited her height, her slenderness, and her dark wavy hair, although where my hair was unruly, her hair always looked styled. Today her hair was no exception, but she had on a stained apron and part of her lipstick had been bitten off.

"Elaine!" Marlene said. "We were in Omaha today and of course Gillian and I thought it would be unforgivable not to pop in and say hello." Marlene emphasized the word "in."

"Oh, it's definitely wonderful to see you, but you've caught me at an awkward moment. We're having a dinner party for a doctor that will hopefully sign on at David's clinic, and I want everything to be just right." The phone rang and my mother rolled her eyes. "It has just been one interruption after another," she said as she went in the house and indicated that we should follow. Marlene and I stepped into the cool foyer and followed her to the living room where she picked up the cordless phone. Marlene made admiring sounds and pointed toward the wall arrangements. I crossed my arms and waited for my mother to get off the phone so I could tell her we were leaving.

"What do you mean? Cows are sacred and I wasn't sure about pork, so I decided to serve fish," my mother's voice had lost its usual decorum. Marlene stopped looking at the décor and my arms dropped to my side. My mother listened for a minute and then said tersely, "I'll see what I can do." She slammed the cordless back into its cradle.

"What's wrong?" I asked.

"Everything," she said curtly. She strode into the kitchen and Marlene and I followed. "The doctor," she continued, "and his wife are from India. They do not eat any meat, only dairy products. I was serving salmon steaks."

"How soon will they get here?" Marlene asked.

"Sixty minutes and the first course was to be shrimp bisque," my mother pulled a cover off a stock pot on the stove and fished a shrimp out of the soup with a slotted spoon. She threw the shrimp into the sink.

"Now, Elaine, you don't want to waste perfectly good shrimp," Marlene said, a hint of panic in her voice.

"You aren't thinking of serving them that soup after you've taken the shrimp out?" I asked. "What if you miss one?"

"I don't have much of a choice," my mother said, flinging another shrimp into the sink.

"But Mom," I said, "if they're not eating meat or fish for religious reasons, wouldn't it upset them to find a shrimp in the soup?"

"Gillian has a point," Marlene nodded. "You don't want to take chances with someone's immortal soul."

My mother stopped and looked at Marlene. "What exactly would you suggest I do? Order a cheese pizza?"

"We can just start over," Marlene said brightly.

"Start over?" My mother waved the slotted spoon. "We've got," she stopped and looked at the clock, "an hour!"

"What were you going to serve with the salmon?" Marlene asked.

"Asparagus spears," my mother said hesitantly. "And the steaks were going to have sautéed mushrooms in a cream sauce."

"Canned or fresh mushrooms?" Marlene asked.

"Fresh. They're sliced and ready to be sautéed."

"Do you have anything for salad?" Marlene asked.

"I was serving soup because salad is so common, but, yes, there's romaine lettuce in the fridge," my mother said.

"But it's salad weather, not soup weather," Marlene said. "Do you have tomatoes?"

"There are two on the counter behind you."

"And you have some pasta or noodles?"

"A whole cupboard of pasta," my mother responded.

"Perfect!" Marlene said.

My mother turned to me. "Did she say perfect?"

Marlene waved a hand at my mother. "I'll just throw together a creamy mushroom sauce for the pasta, we'll have buttered asparagus spears on the side, and a nice salad with the romaine and the tomatoes. Everything will be fine."

"What about dessert?" I asked.

"Dessert is done," my mother said. "I've got a chocolate torte with raspberry sauce. And I've got dinner rolls from the bread shop that we could warm up."

"Where do you keep the pasta?" Marlene asked.

"In here," my mother opened a cupboard. "Gillian, would you please get six salad plates from the top cupboard and bring them to the dining room? Oh, and you'd better wash them first, they haven't been used in a while. I'll see to the rest of the table."

My heart melted as I watched my mother walk out of the room. She wanted six salad plates. She *had* planned on Marlene and I for dinner. And I had been on the verge of leaving because I thought she had implied we would ruin everything.

I washed the cream colored plates with gold trim while my mother bustled in and out of the kitchen and answered Marlene's questions about the kinds of cheeses and spices that were on hand. I took the plates into the dining room and put them on the table. The dining room walls are painted a rose color. My mother had chosen a darker rose table cloth with a flower arrangement of green ferns and lilies. It was beautiful.

"No, no," my mother came into the room. "Don't set those plates out yet. We'll chill the plates and I'll put the salad on them right before everyone is seated." I started to pick up one of the plates when she grabbed my arm. "Gillian, I'm a little worried." She looked toward the kitchen. "I offered her cookbooks for the pasta sauce and she said she was going to 'wing it.'"

I patted my mother's arm. "Don't worry. She doesn't need them. Everything will be fine."

We went back into the kitchen where Marlene was pouring three glasses of wine. "Elaine, you seemed a tad stressed and since you have so much wine on hand, I thought we'd just have a small glass to put us in a more festive mood. Of course, just a tiny bit for Gillian since she's driving and," Marlene paused, looked at me, and held a wine glass up, "she has a little announcement to make."

"Announcement?" my mother asked.

Marlene nodded and held the glass a little higher. "Baby announcement."

"Really?" My mother looked at me. "You're pregnant?"

I felt my pulse beat in my ear. "I'm not pregnant, but Clint and I have been talking about adoption."

"A baby is a baby." Marlene winked at me. "Your mother will want to hear all about your plans."

"Actually, right now," my mother paused and looked at the mushrooms sautéing and the water bubbling for the pasta, "I think I might take my wine with me while I change clothes."

"Of course," Marlene said, sounding slightly miffed.

"Can I help you with anything?" I asked Marlene after my mother went upstairs.

"Oh, I suppose we should find a container for that soup. It should be in the refrigerator. And does your mother have a nice big serving bowl for the pasta?"

I rummaged through the cupboards and found a container. I went to the dining room hutch for a serving bowl that matched the china when I heard a car pull up in the drive. I glanced out the window and saw the car had parked by the curb. I took the bowl to Marlene. "I think the company is here. I'm going upstairs to tell Mom."

There are four bedrooms upstairs, or I should say there were four bedrooms, because at the top of the stairs I could see my old room had been turned into a home office. I walked down the hall and knocked on the door of the master bedroom. "Mom," I said. "They're here."

"They're fifteen minutes early." My mother opened the door. She was dressed in a sleeveless black and white pantsuit. She walked down the hall into my old room and looked out the window. The window faced the front of the house and we both looked down and saw Vincent.

"Vincent!" I said.

"He's always early," my mother said, putting in an earring. "Aren't doctors supposed to be late?"

"Mom!" I said. "You said the doctor you were entertaining was from India!"

"He is. But, Gillian, you know Vincent is head of the medical staff at David's clinic so of course he would be coming to dinner to meet the new doctor, too. Now come on, let's go check on things in the kitchen. I've got to thank Marlene for everything she's done."

I remained rooted in front of the window watching Vincent check out the license plate on Marlene's car. Vincent has black hair and an attractive face. A woman in a navy blue sheath with sleek dark hair suddenly appeared by his side and linked her arm through his and with sudden clarity I knew I was looking at salad plates five and six.

I dashed to the bathroom, closed the door and took stock of my unruly hair, rumpled tank top and wrinkled shorts in the full length mirror. I unbuttoned my shorts and pulled my tank top down. It looked better. I rummaged through the top drawer and found mascara, which I applied liberally and lip gloss, which I applied lightly. I combed my hair and checked myself in the mirror. The tank top was rumpled again. I found safety pins in the bottom drawer of the vanity. I pulled the tank down and pinned it to my panties on both sides. I buttoned up my shorts and looked in the mirror. I couldn't believe it. I turned from side to side. With the tank top pulled down, the top of my bra showed and I had cleavage. Really good cleavage.

"Gillian," my mother called from downstairs and I jumped. I shut the drawer and straightened my shorts. I'd leave the tank pinned. All I had to do was walk downstairs, say goodbye, grab Marlene and I'd be out of there. Why should I even care what Vincent thought? He'd never contacted me after the divorce, not even to ask about my progress. I didn't know what I'd ever seen in him.

"Gillian," my mother called, slightly louder this time.

"Coming," I called back. I went to the top of the stairs and took a deep breath. I put my hand on the banister and began to walk down. Everyone was waiting at the bottom.

"Gillian?" my mother said.

"You changed your top," Marlene said.

Vincent looked up. "Gillian."

I reached the bottom of the stairs. "Hello, Vincent," I said.

The woman in the sheath looked back and forth between Vincent and I.

"I just can't believe it," he said, staring at me. "I didn't think I'd ever see," he paused. Marlene gasped and put a hand to her chest and my mother raised her eyebrows, "you walking so well," he finished the sentence.

A timer went off in the kitchen. "Oh dear, the pasta's done," Marlene said, looking worriedly between Vincent and myself before hurrying into the kitchen.

"No, wait, I'll take care of it," my mother said, as she followed Marlene.

"Where is the bathroom?" the woman in the blue sheath asked.

"Down the hall, to the right," I said.

"Gillian," Vincent said, after the woman had gone down the hall, "could I ask you to do something for me?"

My heart thudded in my chest. "What?" I asked.

"Would you take a few steps forward and then walk back?"

I walked across the foyer and then walked back to Vincent by the stairway. He knelt down to look at my left ankle.

"I never thought your ankle would heal this well," he said. "I wouldn't even see the scars if I weren't looking for them."

After my accident, the surgeon had jovially described that putting my ankle back together was the equivalent of doing a jigsaw puzzle, except the pieces were inside my leg. Vincent, in his first year of residency at the time, had not really stated an opinion other than to make sure I went to a rehabilitation hospital in Lincoln, offering that it was better for the type of injury I had sustained. In hindsight, I thought it had probably been a better place for him to serve divorce papers. Vincent was still probing my ankle and I looked down at the top of his dark hair and wondered what we'd ever had in common.

"Could you lift your foot up please?" he asked.

I blew hair away from my forehead and did as he asked.

"Gillian?" he asked.

"What?" I answered. He had placed my foot back on the floor and his index and middle finger moved up the back of my leg. His fingers stopped at my knee but a bolt of electricity kept going upwards and I suddenly remembered at least one thing we had in common.

"Gillian!" my mother's voice was followed by her stiletto heels.

"I was just examining her ankle," Vincent said, almost stumbling backward in his hurry to stand.

"Gillian," my mother repeated. "Marlene insists that you're both staying for dinner!"

"Oh, no!" I said.

"What do you mean 'oh, no?'" my mother demanded. "She'll leave if you tell her to, won't she?"

"I'll see what I can do," I said.

The dining room table easily accommodated eight, rather than the planned six. My step-father, David, sat at the head of the table. He has thinning blond hair, sharp blue eyes, and an internal anger that always seemed to be in a simmering stage whenever I was present. My mother and Marlene were seated on either side of him while I sat between my mother and the doctor's wife. Across from me were Vincent and his date. The doctor sat at the other end of the table.

Mrs. Singh, the doctor's wife, wore a sleeveless, gold blouse trimmed in wine-colored rick-rack. Over her shoulder was a gold satin sash with designs in the same wine color. "This pasta is delicious," she said.

"Thank you," Marlene and my mother responded at the same time.

I noticed little spots of red had appeared on my step-father's cheeks.

An uncomfortable silence followed which was broken by Marlene. "I have been shopping for dresses all afternoon," she said to Mrs. Singh, "and I did not see any as beautiful as the one you are wearing."

"Thank you," Mrs. Singh answered.

"Sari," my mother leaned across the table and corrected Marlene in a low voice.

Marlene wiped her lips with her napkin and waved a hand at my mother. "Oh, now Elaine, there is absolutely no need to apologize."

The red circles on my step-father's cheeks expanded. "I should say not," he huffed.

"I think," the woman in the sheath said to Vincent, "that I deserve an apology, or at least an explanation. I have yet to be introduced to your ex-wife."

Dr. Singh looked around the table. "Ex-wife?" he asked.

"You weren't introduced?" Vincent asked.

"No," I said.

"Stephanie, this is Gillian. Gillian, this is Stephanie," Vincent said quickly.

"I thought," Dr. Singh said slowly, "that Gillian was one of your daughters."

"She is my step-daughter," David said.

"My daughter from a previous marriage," my mother said.

"Gillian used to be married to him," Marlene pointed across the table at Vincent, "but now she's married to my son, Clint."

"And you live nearby?" Dr. Singh asked.

"No, we live in Bend Brook," Marlene said. "It's not far from the Kansas border."

"They just dropped by unannounced," my step-father said.

Spots of pink appeared on Marlene's cheeks. "Family is never unannounced," she said to David before addressing Mrs. Singh again. "The reason I was shopping for a new dress is because my granddaughter has the lead in the church musical this Friday night."

"What is she in?" Mrs. Singh asked.

"A musical. It's a play where you sing," Marlene said.

"Ahhh," Mrs. Signh said.

"Yes, we are very proud of her. And Gillian is the Jackson County Probation Officer. She had to be in Omaha today to talk to someone after we had a murder in Bend Brook this past week."

"Who was murdered?" Stephanie asked.

"The county attorney," Marlene said. "Gillian knew him very well."

"Is that true?" my mother asked. "You knew him well?"

"I knew him," I said. "We worked in the same courthouse."

"I read about the murder in the paper," Vincent said.

"It was on the nightly news, too," Stephanie said.

"Gillian found the body," Marlene said.

"You did?" Vincent asked.

"Yes," I said.

"Wow," said Stephanie.

Marlene nodded. "Gillian's car is part of the crime scene, so we had to take my car today."

"He died in your car?" Vincent asked.

"That sounds like the television program with the special victims unit," Dr. Singh said.

"He didn't die in my car," I said. "I was at his house. My car was in the driveway, so it's marked off as part of the crime scene."

There were several simultaneous "ahhhhs" around the room.

"It does sound like the television program we watch," Mrs. Singh said.

"You were at his house?" Vincent asked.

"What killed him?" Dr. Singh asked.

"He may have been hit on the back of the head," I said.

"But couldn't you tell? Aren't you studying to be a doctor?" Mrs. Singh asked.

"No," my step-father said. "That's our oldest daughter, Melanie. She's in medical school and Shannon, the youngest, is a violinist."

"Gillian is my oldest daughter," my mother said.

Marlene cleared her throat and addressed Vincent. "Gillian was at Trent Green's house to pick up some police reports that he had taken home with him. Isn't that right, Gillian?"

"Yes," I said, glancing at Vincent. "I was there because of work."

My step-father cleared his throat. "I'm sure this all sounds rather unusual to you," he said to Dr. Singh. He gave Marlene a stern look, "Most families don't announce their personal business at dinner."

"No, no, we understand about these family situations." Mrs. Singh said. "Dr. Singh and I have been watching reality shows on TV, too. We like the one with the eighteen children very much, but your family is very interesting, too, especially now that you have this murder."

The simmering anger in my step-father appeared to be coming to a rolling boil. He clutched his water glass and took a sip. "I believe Gillian is the only member of this group who would find herself associated with a murder. It would seem she has chosen somewhat of a Bohemian lifestyle."

Marlene's fork hit the table. "I will have you know," she said with the same intensity as my step-father, "that Bend Brook is comprised of German and Irish descendents."

"Look at the time," I said and glanced at my watch. "I think we'll have to pass on dessert."

FIFTEEN

Clint had also noticed my "new" tank top when I got home and an hour later we were in bed, listening to a light rain against the window.

"I had a talk with Brandon Delaney today," Clint said.

"You did?" I sat up. Brandon Delaney was the former boyfriend of Jessica Coffers and the father of Logan.

Clint sat up, too. "Well, sort of a talk. His dad came into The Implement this morning and I saw Brandon standing outside by their pickup so I went over just to feel him out about whether he was ever going to want to have a relationship with Logan."

"He's just a kid, too," I said. "How he feels about a relationship with Logan could change in a couple of years."

"Yeah, it could. But I just wanted to know how things stood right now. So I went up to him and said 'you know, my wife and I are interested in adopting Logan.' And he shrugged and said, 'Good for you.' So I said, 'it would make me feel a lot better if you'd send in the paperwork so we'd know you weren't going to pursue any parental right to Logan.'"

"Actually," I said, "according to Mary Lee, his lack of response has put him out of the loop as far as Logan. And she said neither the Banners nor Jessica wanted to pursue child support."

"Yeah, but listen, he didn't say anything for a little bit and then he said, 'I don't have any rights to that kid.' And I said, 'as the biological father you would have rights along with the responsibility.' He didn't say anything for a little bit and then he said, 'that kid's not mine.' After that Brandon's dad came out of The Implement and then they both got in the truck and left."

I got out of bed and pulled my robe on. "That might be an eighteen-year-old's way of saying he doesn't want the responsibility of a child."

"I took it as his way of saying that Logan wasn't his kid, so after I got off work I went and had a talk with Josh." Josh was Ashley's older brother and in the same class as both Brandon and Jessica.

"What did Josh say?" I asked.

"He said it was Jessica that broke up with Brandon somewhere between basketball and prom. Josh said Brandon took it really hard and Jessica wouldn't tell him why she dumped him."

"Between basketball and prom?" I questioned. "Logan was born in August so she would have been . . ." Clint and I both counted on our fingers.

"Let's say basketball is in January, Clint said.

"And prom is in April," I said. We both counted on our fingers again.

"She probably got pregnant in January," I said. "Logan could very well be Brandon's child."

"Brandon seemed pretty adamant, sort of like he was hurt about the whole thing," Clint said.

"It would make more sense for Brandon to break up with Jessica if he found out she was pregnant," I said. "Unless she was afraid to tell the Banners. She might have not wanted Brandon to realize she was pregnant and breaking up with him would have been a way to do that. And . . ." I paused.

"And?" Clint asked.

"And she never told me that Brandon wasn't the father. I think Jessica would have confided in me about something like that," I said.

"Does she talk to you a lot?" Clint asked.

"Of course she does. I see her every week," I said.

"And she confides in you about personal stuff?"

"Actually, she mainly talks about Logan," I admitted.

"Josh doesn't think Brandon's the father, either," Clint said softly.

I looked over at Clint. "What makes him think that?" I asked.

"Josh said that first of all, Brandon said they never did anything and secondly when Jessica broke up with him, Brandon asked Jessica what he'd done. Josh said now Brandon thinks there was another boyfriend all along. Someone from her past."

"I don't think she would have been able to see anyone on the side. I think Mitch and Kay would have known about it."

"Well, there's more. This is just Josh's theory, but he doesn't think Jessica is Logan's mother. He said Jessica had good friends at one of the group homes she lived at in Louisiana. One of those girls was moving to Nebraska and was supposed to call Jessica last spring and they were going to hookup. Hookup is Josh's term," Clint added.

"I think those are just rumors," I said.

"Josh didn't think so. One of the girls in their class let Jessica use her cell phone number so the Louisiana girl could leave messages."

"Why would Jessica do that? Why wouldn't she just get the calls at the Banner's house?"

Clint shrugged. "Josh thinks the Louisiana girl left the baby under the bridge so Jessica would find it and raise it."

"Is Josh watching too much CSI?" I asked.

Clint smiled. "If you stop to think about it, it would explain how she could have a baby without anyone suspecting she was pregnant."

"But she loves Logan and he wouldn't . . ." I couldn't finish my sentence.

"Have been her own baby?" Clint asked.

I sighed. "Yes."

"But we plan to love a child, even if it's not our own," he said.

"But would we love any child?" I asked.

"I don't know. You do light up when you talk about Logan," Clint said.

"So do you," I sighed. "And so does Jessica. Logan is just a lovable little boy." I moved closer to Clint and put my arms around him with my chin on his shoulder. He took my hand and kissed my wrist in response.

"Clint," I said. "I know we both had our hearts set on Logan, but Jessica really has no reason to put him up for adoption now." I lifted my head, not liking the implication of what I had just said.

"That's true," Clint agreed. "With Trent Green gone, there's really no need for Jessica to give him up."

I grimaced. "I really wish you wouldn't say it that way. It makes it sound like Jessica . . ."

"Had a motive?" Clint finished.

I nodded.

Lightening flashed outside the window followed by a loud crack of thunder. "Coco is going to be scared." Clint said.

"Should we bring her inside?" I asked.

"She needs to learn to be outside." He put a hand on my arm. "You still want to adopt a child even if it's not Logan, don't you?"

I thought for a minute about having a small stranger inhabit our house. Then I thought of Logan putting his little hand around my fingers. "I think we should still adopt, even if it's not Logan," I said.

"And don't worry about the motive thing with Jessica," Clint said. "The other news around town this afternoon is Trent Green's briefcase was found in a ditch about a mile and a half from his house."

"Why didn't you tell me this before?" I pushed him and he nearly fell out of bed. "What was in that briefcase?"

"Absolutely nothing," Clint said. "There were a couple of pages of some land survey documents blowing around the field, but that was all they found."

"Who announced this?" I asked. "The State Patrol?"

"No, the guy that found it, Jack Lohrmeister. He farms the land. It supports what you said about Trent having police reports that somebody wanted. That should let Jessica off the hook, right?"

I sighed. "I hope so. Newt's just out to get her."

"Never mind Newt," Clint said. "He'll set his sites on someone else pretty soon. Remember when he and Karl were at odds?"

I smiled. "They're still at odds."

Clint took my hand again. "I just want to make sure that we are going to go ahead with adopting kids, right?"

"Did you say kids as in plural?" I asked, a little panicked.

"I just meant one, at least one at a time," Clint said. "You're sure about this, though?" Clint asked.

I thought about it for a minute. "Yes, I'm sure," I said.

"Good, because we've got those training films in Lincoln on Tuesday afternoon and some lady left a message on our answering machine today to remind us about the home visit Wednesday afternoon."

A crack of thunder reverberated throughout the house and the rain began in earnest.

"I hope Coco doesn't dig herself out," Clint said.

"Maybe we'd better bring her inside," I said.

Clint got up and grabbed his jeans. "It would be better than chasing her around the country in the middle of the night."

"We could put her kennel out on the porch," I said. "I don't want Coco to wreck the house before Wednesday."

An hour later we were back in bed. There was the faint smell of skunk in the air and the bed was shaking. I felt something cold and moist press against my bare stomach. I put my hand on Coco's nose and pushed her over to Clint's side.

"This dog, I swear she's more trouble than she's worth," Clint said, digging Coco out from under the covers and putting her back on top of the blanket. Thunder cracked and Coco burrowed over to Clint's side of the bed. "Eeeesh. She's drooling on me," Clint said. "I think we made a big mistake," he said.

"I know. We should have left her in her kennel," I said.

Thunder boomed in the distance and the bed shook even harder. I heard Clint sigh wistfully from his side of the bed.

"What's the matter?" I asked.

"Coco will never be a hunting dog," he said.

SIXTEEN

"How much mascara are you going to put on?" Clint glanced at me in the bathroom mirror as he dragged a razor down the side of his cheek.

"A lot, I guess," I checked my eyelashes in the mirror and put the mascara wand back in the tube. "I just can't seem to concentrate. That news about Logan's father is so . . ."

"I know," Clint nodded, rinsing his razor under the faucet, "it would just be one more issue we'd have to face if Jessica ever decided we could adopt him."

I sighed. My concern about the possibility of Logan's father being an unknown entity was for an entirely different reason than Clint's. Hadn't I done Jessica's pre-sentence investigation? Didn't I talk to her each and every week? If Brandon wasn't Logan's father, I should have known about it before now.

"What's the matter?" Clint asked and his eyes met mine in the bathroom mirror.

"It's just that I thought Jessica would have confided in me," I said. "I thought she saw me as someone who wouldn't judge her." I shrugged. "I'm sure she didn't view me as a friend, but I thought at least I was. . ."

"A port in the storm?" Clint asked.

"That's a good way to describe it." I said. "I thought she saw me as someone she could trust."

Clint rinsed shaving residue off his face. "We'll have to discuss this later. We're going to be late for church."

"I'm going to skip church this morning," I said.

"Oh?" Clint questioned.

"Remember that retired police officer in Lincoln? He wanted a description of JoJo's assailant and I told him I'd give him a call after I talked to Lark." I said. "I was going to call him yesterday but then your mom and I stayed in Omaha later than we planned."

"Did you forget we're going to Mom and Dad's for lunch?" Clint asked.

I hadn't forgotten, Marlene had reminded me several times that she was expecting us for a family dinner after church. "Could you just pick me up after church?" I asked.

Once Clint had driven away, I took my cell phone and the paper with Sid's numbers outside and sat on the porch steps. I filled Coco's water bowl and poured some dog chow for her. She drank thirstily and then ignored the food in favor of bringing me her ball. She was full of energy after last night's storm even if I wasn't. I punched in the number.

"I was waiting for your call," Sid Weissman said. I heard a drawer open and papers being shuffled. "Okay, this time I've got my questions ready. Let's get started and see if your guy matches the one in my cases. What kind of mask?"

"He wore panty hose on his head and a scarf over the panty hose," I said.

"I've got all the standards here, ski mask, Halloween mask, and panty hose with a lone ranger mask over the eyes. The bottom line is his head was fully covered, so I'm counting that as a match. What did he wear?"

"Dark pants and a light colored shirt," I said.

"Tucked in?" Sid asked.

"I don't know. I didn't ask," I said. "But Sid, hold on for a minute, the roommate said JoJo knew who it was. JoJo told her he seemed familiar at the time but then she went home for a visit a couple of years later and she saw him at church and recognized him as the person who tried to rape her."

There was complete silence on the other end. "Sid, are you there?" I asked.

"Yeah, yeah, I'm here. That just sort of floored me. Did she go to the authorities?"

"No, she said that he was with his wife and she didn't want to upset his wife."

"Oh, jeez. Well she fits right in with my other victims," Sid said.

"How so?" I asked.

"The guy I'm looking for chooses victims who'll do what they're told and won't talk back. Women that don't want to make a fuss and draw attention to themselves. I had him profiled way back when these cases were hot. The guy I'm looking for probably has areas in his life where he's not in control, so he chooses victims that will do what they're told."

"He'd have to know them beforehand to understand their personality," I said.

"You got it," Sid said. "I was thinking maybe a teacher, a scout leader, somebody that has a lot of contact with the kids."

I inhaled sharply.

"What?" Sid asked.

"It's just a thought, something that came to my mind," I said.

"Say it," Sid said.

"Pastor Jim at our church is very involved with the kids and," I stopped again.

"Gillian! Stop doing that and tell me what's going on," Sid said.

I choked a bit. "Pastor Jim was one of the people who heard me say our county attorney had police reports on the other Bend Brook cases. He offered to go with me to Trent's house. He was even sort of pushy about it."

Silence.

"Sid?" I said.

"I'm here." he said. "You just said he was 'one of the people' who heard you were looking for those police reports. So there were other people who heard this, too? What did you do, announce it at church?"

"There were three people who heard. Pastor Jim and his assistant, Scott, and the county judge were all there."

I heard a drawer slam. "Okay, okay, give me the full names of everyone who heard that the county attorney had police reports on JoJo's assault. I'm going to run background checks."

I gave Sid the names and what limited information I knew on each of them.

"I got a few more questions," Sid said. "Do you think your Pastor Jim would have known JoJo back then?"

Hadn't Pastor Jim said he'd counseled Georgia Lohrmeister over her daughter? "Yes, he would have," I said.

"Is your Pastor Jim an overly friendly type of guy or is he an odd duck?"

"I don't know, a little of both. He's sort of geeky." I said.

"Does he still have contact with kids?" Sid asked.

"Of course," I said. "He does a church musical every summer, among other things. My niece has the lead in the musical this year."

"How often do you see your niece?" Sid asked.

"I'll see her this afternoon," I said.

"Talk to her," Sid said. "See what she thinks of the good Pastor. Sometimes kids have a sixth sense and they know that somebody's a pervert, but they just don't know how to say it or who to tell." He paused. "Unless she's the type of kid who'd scream and yell if you looked at her cross-eyed."

"No," I said. "She's a quiet kid who doesn't like people to fuss over her."

I heard Sid breathe over the phone. "Talk to her. And then call me back."

SEVENTEEN

"Mother, you've outdone yourself," my father-in-law forked up a piece of fried chicken from the platter on the dining room table.

"Oh, Frank," Marlene waved a hand at him from the other end of the table. "You're just saying that because it's your favorite meal."

"Is this really your favorite meal, Grandpa?" Josh asked. "My favorite meal is Taco Bell."

"Josh, I could eat your Grandma's fried chicken, mashed potatoes, and cucumbers in cream every day of my life and you'd not hear one complaint out of me."

Linda, Clint's sister, pushed her chair back from the table. "And don't forget, we have angel food cake and strawberries for dessert. Ashley, do you want to help me bring the dessert in here?"

"I'll help Ashley with the cake," I said, wanting to find a moment alone with her.

"Can we hold off on the dessert so I at least have a fighting chance to finish my chicken?" Frank asked.

"I don't want anyone to leave the table," Marlene said, getting up from her chair, "until you've seen the dresses I bought yesterday. I can't decide which one I should wear to the musical this Friday."

"Is the musical this Friday?" Clint winked at me.

"Clint!" Marlene said. "Don't you dare forget about the musical! I'm saving front row seats for the whole family."

Ashley rolled her eyes.

"Mom," Linda said, "why don't you try the dresses on? We'll get the dessert ready while you change."

"That's a good idea," I said.

As it turned out, time alone with Ashley was nixed when everyone helped clear the table. Coffee and dessert were on the table when Marlene walked into the dining room. She held up an arm and said, "ta da!" The dress parted at the bosom and Linda winced. It was a shapeless blue dress with a white inset across the shoulders and sleeves. It buttoned up the front with excessively large white buttons. "Well?" Marlene asked.

"It has a lot of blue," Clint offered.

"The color contrast is nice," Linda said.

"Blue's a very becoming color on you," Rosalee, Clint's Aunt, chimed in.

"The buttons seem a bit overpowering," I said.

Marlene frowned. "I don't usually buy button-up dresses, but this was a size smaller than what I normally wear."

"Well, we can't make a decision until we've seen the other dress," Frank said.

I could tell by everyone's expressions what a relief the other dress was to us all. A black skirt and an iridescent sage tunic with a v-neck was much more becoming.

"I like this dress a lot better, Grandma," Ashley said.

"But see how sparkly the top is? It's covered with sequins," Marlene said.

"What shoes would you wear with it?" Linda asked.

"Those black heels with the open toe," my mother-in-law responded.

"I think that's the dress you should wear," I said.

"You don't think it's too flashy?" Marlene asked and we all shook our heads.

After we finished with dishes, Ashley seemed to disappear. "Where's Ashley?" I asked Linda.

"She and Mom went out to get something from the refrigerator in the garage just a minute ago," Linda said.

I went outside and found Marlene pulling weeds in the flower bed. "Do you know what happened to Ashley?" I asked.

"I gave her some meat to feed the kittens under the corncrib," Marlene said.

The barn was directly across from the house. Two corn cribs and a Quonset hut were at a diagonal to the house and the barn. Ashley was sitting on the ground about fifteen feet away from one of the corncribs. I walked over to her. "Mind if I join you?" I asked.

She looked up at me with smoldering blue eyes outlined by long black lashes. "Okay, but you have to be quiet until they come out," she said.

I sat down by her and she threw a piece of meat that landed midway between us and the corncrib. A tiny kitten face peeked out from underneath the corncrib. The kitten hesitated and then came out from under the corncrib. Two other kittens appeared and watched as the first one moved slowly toward the meat. Ashley and I sat motionless while the kitten slowly and warily moved toward the meat, grabbed it and ran back to the corncrib, its fat gray tail pointed straight up so that it looked like an elongated triangle.

"That all-gray one's the bravest," Ashley said, breaking the silence. "Grandma's been leaving them bread and water in the morning, but she said they won't come out at all while she's around."

"Shouldn't they be with their mother yet?" I asked.

"Grandma said it has been a couple of days since she's seen the mother cat." Ashley took another piece of meat and threw it.

I hadn't quite thought of a subtle way to broach the subject of Pastor Jim. "So how's the musical going?" I asked.

Ashley's shoulders sagged. "I'm so sick of that stupid musical. I'll be so glad when it's over."

"You aren't enjoying it?" I asked, surprised at her response.

Ashley shrugged in response.

"Is Pastor Jim unpleasant or does he ever seem a little strange to you?" I asked.

"Pastor Jim?" She turned to look at me. "He's always really strange. Are you just figuring that out now, Aunt Gillian?"

"I wasn't really talking about eccentricities. I wondered if he treated you differently." So much for subtleness, I told myself.

Ashley threw another piece of meat to the kittens, her mouth pursed in consternation. "You've heard the rumors, haven't you?"

"Rumors?" I repeated, feeling my heartbeat picking up speed. "What rumors?"

"Well," Ashley swiped hair away from her face with her hand. "Madison O'Malley says the only reason I got the lead in the musical is because Grandma always sucks up to Pastor Jim." I looked over at Ashley and saw her bottom lip tremble. "She told everyone I wouldn't have gotten the lead if I weren't Pastor Jim's little pet."

"First of all," I said, "I can't quite picture your Grandma sucking up to anyone," I saw the lips turn up in a small smile at that, "and secondly, Madison O'Malley should have tried out herself before she started accusing people of playing favorites."

"Oh, but she did try out! And she's really good and everybody knows it!" Outbursts weren't the norm for the usually quiet Ashley and a glance at her face told me how upset she was about the Madison O'Malley situation.

"But Pastor Jim chose you. He must have had a reason," I said, inwardly thinking his reasoning might have a criminal aspect to it.

"I went and talked to him about it because Madison was making such a big deal about everything," Ashley said.

"And?" I said.

"And he said Madison has one of the best voices in the congregation, and he said he was including the adults, too, but she wasn't always dependable. He said he had to look at the big picture and not just who had the best voice. And then . . ." Ashley stopped talking as two of the kittens approached the food and we waited until they'd gotten it and gone back under the corncrib.

"And then?" I asked.

"Well, then Madison went and talked to him. She said that being a good two years older than me should count for something, but he said he couldn't have a lead with such a wonderful voice that it would overpower everyone else in the whole musical." Ashley gave me a sideways glance. "Or at least that's what she says."

"You both talked to Pastor Jim alone?" I asked.

"Yeah," Ashley nodded.

"What was your impression of him when you were alone? Did he act differently?"

Ashley shrugged. "He was just his usual self. He told me not to worry and then he made some stupid jokes that no one but him thinks are funny and then I had to wait a really long time while he found a Bible verse."

"Why was he looking for a Bible verse?"

"He gives every kid that comes to talk to him a Bible verse. And he always starts out with, 'now I've tried to reach you on your level,' and he'll point to those stupid shoes if he's got them on, and then he'll say 'and now I want you to try to reach God on his level.' And then he gives out a Bible verse. Mine was about finding strength. Madison's was about making a joyful noise to the Lord and she's been making dumb noises at practice ever since." Ashley flung a piece of meat at the corncrib. "And that's not the worst of it."

"What's the worst of it?" I asked.

"She learned all my parts and she's been singing them and everybody can see she's a lot better than me so last week I went to Pastor Jim and told him I wanted to switch with Madison. I told him she could have the lead."

"What did Pastor Jim say?" I asked.

"He said no! And he told Scott not to tolerate anymore bad behavior from Madison and then Pastor Jim himself went over to Madison at practice, and he didn't give her a Bible verse or tie it into God or anything, he just said 'knock it off and I mean now.'"

"And has she?" I asked.

"She has around them, but she's gotten all her friends to be mean to me now, too, so I try to stay by Josh because they won't say anything in front of him."

"I didn't think Josh was in the musical," I said.

Ashley sniffed. "He's on props so he doesn't have to be there every single minute. Anyway, last week Pastor Jim said everything would be better, but so far it has only gotten worse. He should have let me switch with Madison."

"Ashley," I said, "Pastor Jim was right when he wouldn't let you switch. There are going to be other Madison O'Mallys in this world and you can't let them control what you can and cannot do in life."

Ashley wiped her nose. She tore up some of the meat that was still left and then looked over at me. "At least this musical's only ninety minutes long. Last year *David and the Technicolor Coat* was way over two hours."

"So if this musical starts at seven o'clock, you'll be done and out of there before you know it," I said.

"And afterward I'm going to spend the night at my friend Ellie's house. She's got some fireworks saved from last year and her mom said we can shoot them off. At least I have that to look forward to," she threw another piece of meat.

"Hey!"

We both started and looked across the farm yard to see my father-in-law coming over to us, his dog Beau at his side. "Are you feeding those kittens the chopped ham that I order special from the butcher?"

"Grandma said I could," Ashley said. "She wants me to tame them down."

He shook his head. "And she's picked my lunch meat to tame them."

Ashley smiled. "She said if you'd have spent an hour with them every day when they were born, they'd already be tame."

"Well, you can tell your grandma I am not going to be the babysitter for a bunch of damned cats," he said.

"Language, Grandpa!" Ashley said. "Remember, it's Sunday."

"Well, there'll be more language where that came from if those cats tame down so much that I can't walk across the yard without them running between my feet."

We all looked at the kittens that had taken refuge underneath the corn crib.

"I think it'll be a long time before they're anywhere near your feet," I said.

"Do you think the mother cat is ever coming back?" Ashley asked.

"Well, I think it has been a good three days since I seen her," Frank said. "Something must of got her, most likely a coyote. Those coyotes have been yipping it up in the back pasture every night for the past week." He looked toward the corncrib. "Too bad, she was a good mouser." He pointed at the meat Ashley was holding. "I probably won't be able to say the same thing about her kittens, though."

"They'll be good mousers, too, but they aren't going to come out again until Beau leaves." Ashley looked at the dog who was watching the meat. She threw him a piece and Beau caught it in his mouth.

"So you're going to eat my lunch meat, too?" Frank said to the dog, who wagged his tail apologetically. "Too many animals to feed, if you ask me. Which reminds me, I've got chores to do." We watched them walk toward the barn, Beau's old hips moving from side to side. A cat sat in the door of the barn and rubbed against Frank's leg when he walked inside.

"Isn't it odd," I said to Ashley, "that these kittens are wild while the cats in the barn are tame?"

"If these kittens had been born in the barn, they'd be tame, too," Ashley said.

"Simply by being born in the barn?" I asked.

Ashley shrugged. "They'd see Grandpa every single day when he goes in and out of the barn."

"But the kittens under the corncrib can see the house and the people who come and go everyday, just like the barn cats."

"Yeah, but if they'd been in the barn Grandpa would have picked them up when they were born and I would of got a call from him where he would of said, 'We've got kittens in the barn who've just opened their eyes and your grandma and I are fresh out of names for them. You'd better get over here and do something about it.'" Ashley had changed her voice to mimic Frank.

I laughed. "That was a pretty good imitation of your grandpa, but I still don't understand why the barn kittens are tame and these aren't."

Ashley threw the last piece of chopped ham and we watched as the all-gray kitten warily made his way to the meat, slowly followed by the other two. Ashley stood up and brushed off the back of her shorts and they all ran back under the corncrib. "These kittens see people everyday," Ashley said, "but they weren't really *raised* by people. You see, Aunt Gillian, it's two totally different things. It'll be a long time before these kittens trust anyone."

The gray kitten stuck its head out and watched us from the safety of the corncrib. "Thanks, Ashley," I said looking up at her. "I think I understand that now."

EIGHTEEN

My car was finally released and I picked it up on Monday morning before work. I called Sid on my way to the courthouse and told him about my conversation with Ashley. Sid said he'd get back to me as soon as heard back on the background checks.

Unfortunately, the unexpected morning routine had made me uncharacteristically late. Karl Kittman was my first appointment of the day and when I saw the pickup truck with Lizzie in the back, I knew Karl was unusually early. I reached the door to the courthouse and took the stairs at a trot, only to stop abruptly several steps from the top. A group of people stood outside the glass door that led to the second floor offices.

"It's Gillian!" Karl yelled. He would have thrown his arms up had he not been holding a box of red potatoes.

"There you are!" Dot said in an accusing voice.

"Someone better go tell Newt, before the State Patrol gets here," Dorcas said.

"Newt went to call them when we realized you weren't here," Judy added.

"For being a few minutes late?" I said in disbelief, coming up the last few steps to join the others.

We heard footsteps and turned to see Newt bounding up the steps. First his mouth dropped and then it shut, and he said to me, "So, you decided to come in?"

"I am fifteen minutes late," I said. "It's not a national emergency."

"It's not just that you're late, Gillian," Judy said. "It's the odor that's coming from your office."

I walked over to the glass door, opened it, and inhaled. A very faint and musky, bad-body odor hung in the air.

"Shut that door," Newt said. "It still might be a crime scene!"

"A crime scene?" I asked.

Everyone started talking at once:

"First we noticed the odor . . ."

". . . and your office door was locked, which wasn't unusual . . ."

" . . . and if you were standing right by your office door, hoo boy, it was bad . . ."

". . . Dot went and got a key, but then . . ."

". . . I said you weren't in church yesterday, and no one else here had seen you this weekend either . . ."

". . . then we realized that horrible odor, more of a stench really, was definitely coming from inside your office . . ."

". . . and after what happened to poor Trent Green . . ."

". . . well, we just thought it might be you in there."

"It's onions," I said, belatedly remembering Georgia Lohmeister's directions to keep the onions in a cool, dry place.

I took out my key and walked into the public waiting area. I walked over to my office door and put the key in the keyhole.

"Don't open that door!" Newt bellowed.

"But it's onions," I said, throwing the door open to the gasps of everyone. A blast of warm air permeated with the rank odor drew a simultaneous "Ewwww!" from the assembled crowd. Wilted green onions and festering leeks were on the vegetable exchange table.

Dot stepped in the room beside me. "It's hotter in here than it is outside."

"It always is, if the air conditioner is off," I said. "I'll turn the air conditioner on and it will be Antarctica in less than five minutes."

"I thought they fixed your air conditioner, but" Dot shrugged, "you should have put any leftover vegetables in the refrigerator. Oh, and look, here's a note directing you to do just that."

"At this point they'd better be going in a trash can," Karl said. "I don't want my nice, fresh, red potatoes getting stunk up by those onions."

Newt stepped up to me. "You ignored a direct order not to open the door," he said.

I turned toward Newt. "It's my office and I knew it was onions."

"She certainly would have known it was onions," Dot said, holding her hands up in a see-what-I-have-to-put-up-with gesture. "She ignored written directions to take care of the vegetables."

Karl stepped up to Newt. "You're the one that can't tell the difference between a dead body and an onion gone bad. But I guess you can explain that to the boys from the Patrol."

Heads swung toward Newt to see if Karl's intended barb had made an impact. We all saw that Karl had hit a bull's eye. Newt's mouth formed an O, and with his brown mustache, gave him a look reminiscent of Mr. Potato Head. He teetered on his heels for a minute before hurrying out the door.

"Am I going to be able to get my car licensed today, or do I need to come back?" a woman in the group asked.

"Of course you can license your car, we'll just shut Gillian's door and then it will be business as usual," Dot said.

"I'll help you," Judy said to the woman, walking to the half door that would allow her to take her place behind the counter.

As everyone dispersed, Karl followed me into my office with the box of potatoes. I turned the knob on the air conditioner to high and then turned to Karl. "Would you help me clear these onions away so we can breathe?" I asked.

"You betcha," Karl said. "And you better take these potatoes home if they don't all go out the door today. The only thing that smells worse than an onion gone bad is a potato that's gone bad."

My second appointment of the day was Jessica and I wondered what I could use in place of lunch meat to make her trust me. Jessica came into my office at her appointed time, Logan in her arms. At twenty-two months, Logan seemed as wide across as his mother.

"Should I shut the door, Ma'am?" she said.

"Please do, Jessica," I said, as I settled behind my desk. "Logan must be having a growth spurt, he seems bigger than the last time I saw him."

Jessica smiled at me. "At his eighteen month checkup he weighed twenty-seven pounds," she said. "He's in the ninetieth percentile for his height and eightieth percentile for his weight. The doctor said when he turns two we can double his height and see how tall he's going to be when he's fully grown."

Logan wriggled his way down from Jessica's arms to come around to my side of the desk. I opened the refrigerator and he looked up at me with big blue eyes and a smile. "How about an apple juice today?" I asked.

He nodded and fat little hands wrapped around the juice box. "Tantoo," he said.

"Did he just say thank you?" I asked.

Jessica's smile lit up her face. "It's his newest word." Logan hurried around the desk and climbed onto her lap. I noticed again how thin Jessica was in comparison to Logan's chubbiness. How in the world had she kept her pregnancy a secret?

"Is something the matter, ma'am?" Jessica was watching me.

"I was just noticing how thin you seem in comparison to Logan. You're eating okay?"

"We both eat real good," Jessica said, "we're just complete opposites. I eat in the morning and then if I don't eat anything else all day, I'm okay. Logan isn't a big morning eater but sometimes he eats all afternoon." She looked down at Logan. "I've been giving him carrot sticks when he wants to snack. And listen to him say cucumber. Say cucumber."

Logan shook his head once, keeping the straw in his mouth.

"He can say it," Jessica said, "he just doesn't want to."

"Jessica?" I said.

"Yes, ma'am," she said.

"You know you can trust me," I said.

"Yes, ma'am." she answered.

When she didn't say anything else, I continued. "Is there anything that you'd like to discuss with me? Anything that's been worrying you?"

She watched me with wariness. We listened to Logan slide the straw back and forth in the juice box. "No ma'am," Jessica said.

I sighed. "Jessica, it's clear to me that you want to raise Logan, and Clint and I wouldn't ever adopt Logan without your consent, but what if Logan's father decides that he wants to have Logan as part of his life?"

"He wouldn't ever do that, ma'am," she said.

"But people change," I said, "they grow up, and what might have been a burden at one time is very precious . . ."

"No, ma'am." Jessica had not only interrupted me, but she was firm in the denial. "That would never happen," she said with uncharacteristic finality.

"I wasn't trying to upset you," I said.

She nodded but didn't speak, her eyes now watching every move I made.

"Maybe he'll say cucumber now," I said to try and bring down the tension that had built up in Jessica. We both looked at Logan who was still holding the juice box with one hand and whose eyes had partly closed. Jessica took the juice box from him and placed it on the desk. She turned him over and he snuggled into her shoulder.

"He gets up early most days and sometimes he needs a morning nap," she said.

"I'll turn off the air conditioner so he doesn't catch a chill," I said. I finished with the air conditioner and turned back to Jessica.

"Ma'am, I have a question . . ."

"Yes?" I said, sitting back down at my desk.

"Do you think, I mean is there a chance the police would take Logan away from me?" she asked.

"No," I said. "Why would you even think that?"

She swallowed. "The police came and talked to me," she said.

"Actually," I said, "it was probably the State Patrol. They talked to me, too."

"Because you found Mr. Green," she said.

"Yes, and because they'll talk to everyone who had contact with him before he . . ." I still couldn't say it.

"Died?" she asked quietly.

"Yes," I said. "And I know you were at his office so it would make sense that they'd speak to you."

"He told you about me coming to see him?" the surprise in her voice had made the southern accent more pronounced.

I shrugged. It was senseless to tell her Newt had shared that bit of information with me in a vindictive moment.

"I'm not planning on leaving anymore, if that's what you were asking about before," she said. "And I do think about Logan when I plan things," she finished defiantly.

I picked up a pen and started doodling on my calendar. *Leaving* the pen wrote on its own accord and followed with a question mark. I looked back at Jessica. She stuck her chin out ever so slightly and said in a soft firm voice, "I know what it's like to have a mother in jail and Logan's not going to go through that."

"Jessica," I said. "Why would you think you were going to jail?"

"Trudy March said I was," Jessica's voice had a questioning note.

My back stiffened and I felt hot rage rise in my chest. "Trudy March has overstepped her bounds. Did she say this to you directly? That's harassment and it can be stopped with a protection order." I picked up the phone to call the judge. "Trudy needs to realize where her opinion stops and where your rights begin."

"Ma'am!" Jessica said and a sleepy Logan squirmed at her exclamation. She put him on her other shoulder. "She didn't say anything to me. Mitch was the one who told me she wanted me in jail. I went to ask Mr. Green to see if he was going to file charges."

I put the phone back in the cradle. Jessica was watching me wide-eyed after my little outburst. I looked back at her and noticed that her eyes were especially beautiful today; the blue-green was a rich aqua color. "I overreacted," I said. Mitch had probably wanted Jessica to hear Trudy's opinions from him rather than someone else. I took a deep breath and looked at the word underlined in front of me. "So you planned to leave if you thought you were going to jail?"

She nodded.

"And Logan?"

"I was taking Logan with me," she said.

"And I hope Mr. Green told you that he had no plans to see you in jail," I said.

The worry crease on her brow deepened. "He didn't exactly say that." She paused. "Aunt Kay told me you said he couldn't file any other charges." She paused again and waited for me to confirm this.

"I told your aunt I didn't think he could," I said. "I hope Mr. Green confirmed that."

"Mr. Green said we needed to plan it out so it would come out well for me, and that it would come out well for him, too." Jessica paused. "He didn't really answer my question, he just told me he would handle Trudy March and to leave everything to him."

I leaned back in my chair. "Where were you planning to take Logan?"

Logan stirred and she rubbed his back. She shrugged in response.

"You did have somewhere in mind that you were taking him?"

"Yes, ma'am," she looked off to the side.

"Jessica, look at me please," I said and leaned toward her, "if you ever think about taking Logan to live on the streets, call me, and I will do whatever it takes to keep you both together in a safe environment."

"I wouldn't let him live on the streets," she said, the soft firmness back in her voice.

"Oh?"

"I have. . ." she trailed off.

"You have?" I prompted.

"A friend. A really good friend, like a sister," she said.

"And she'd let you and Logan live with her?" I asked.

"We'd do anything for each other," she said.

"And?" I said.

"And what?" she asked.

"And are you going to tell me more about your friend?"

She paused. "No, ma'am."

I gave her a slight smile. "No matter how many questions I ask?"

"No, ma'am," she returned the smile.

"Then let's set up our time for next week," I said and pulled out my calendar.

I was walking home and giving a little more credence to Josh's theory that Logan might not be Jessica's baby. Maybe Josh was right, after all. If Jessica had a friend that would do anything for her, maybe, just maybe, Jessica would do anything for the friend, including raising that friend's baby. Jessica and Logan had both been taken to the hospital, though. Surely they would have checked Jessica and would have known it was her that had given birth. I stopped in mid-step. Maybe the friend was at the hospital, too, and gave Jessica's name and information instead of her own. I started walking again. Maybe Josh and I were both watching too much TV, but a visit with the doctor would confirm that Jessica had given birth to the child.

My cell phone rang. I checked and saw that it was Sid. "Hello."

"Gillian, are you at a place where you can talk?"

I could tell by Sid's voice he had something. "Yes, I can talk. What did you find out?"

"Well, all three of them have things about them that raise flags."

"You're kidding," I said. "Even the judge?"

"The judge lives with his mother, that's an authoritative female presence," Sid said.

"But he moved back here so he could take care of his mother," I said.

"You get a gold star," Sid said. "He did move back to Bend Brook to take care of his mother. Before he moved in with his mother, he lived in Texas. He moved back here nineteen years ago. Now you do the math."

"Your cases are older," I said.

"Right," Sid said. "He'd would of had a hell of a commute. But he came home often to visit and he knows everyone in town."

"He doesn't fit the physical description, though. I don't know what he looked like when he was younger, but he's a big man."

"Another gold star," Sid said. "So the judge goes to the bottom of the list. Now, on to Scott Torrance. I didn't put it together that he was part of the Montgomery family."

"Is that good or bad?" I asked.

"Good and bad. Good for him because he lives off his wife's money. Bad for him because it's his wife's money. The family donates a lot of stuff, but I doubt if he has any say about it. That, and the fact he works with kids fits the profile of my perp."

"So you think it's Scott?" I asked.

"Did I say it was Scott?" Sid asked. "No, I said they've all got interesting things about them." He stopped and I thought I could hear him licking his lips. "The most interesting by far is Pastor Jim. The Pastor did something that wasn't considered criminal, but made a young girl's parents more than a little uneasy."

"What did he do?"

"He sent this girl notes telling her she was special, one of God's chosen to be exact, and he gave her Bible verses that were meant just for her. Mom found one of the notes, thought it sounded out of place, and called one of the church elders. The elder contacted the police. Pastor Jim said he was trying to improve the girl's self-esteem. The girl said nothing physical happened so that was the end of the story." He paused. "Until now."

"Actually, that sounds a lot like something Pastor Jim would do," I said. "Was this in Bend Brook?"

"No!" Sid barked the answer and I held the phone away from my ear. "This was before he came to Bend Brook. He was with the youth ministry in Nebraska City thirty years ago." Sid enunciated every syllable in the last three words. "My town, my timeline."

I stopped walking again, thinking of the implication of what Sid had just told me. "What now?" I asked.

"Now I need you to do something for me," Sid said. "It's a little complicated. You might have to write it down."

"What exactly do you want me to do?" I asked.

"You said you had a key to JoJo's storage unit?" he asked.

"It's Lark's," I said, "but it has JoJo's things in it. Do you want the address?"

"No. I want Pastor Jim to have the address. I want you to tell him how you went and talked to JoJo's roommate. Then tell him how the roommate saved all of her personal things in a storage unit. Tell him JoJo knew who tried to rape her and it's all written out in a diary. Tell him the diary is at the storage unit and once you get it, you'll know who tried to rape JoJo, not to mention the other victims."

"Sid, wait, you've got it wrong. There's the storage unit in Lincoln, but there's no diary," I said. "Lark never mentioned a diary."

I heard the hiss of the cell phone line and then I could see Sid's thin lips forming the next words. "Gillian, we're setting a trap."

NINETEEN

Sid had also learned that Pastor Jim conducted a Bible study at the Correctional Center in Lincoln on Tuesday night. The study usually ended around 8:30. Sid used that bit of information in his plan, and on Monday afternoon I stopped at Pastor Jim's office to "bait the trap."

Pastor Jim's office is in the hall, located just inside the main door. He was in his office with Scott Torrance.

"Come in, come in," Pastor Jim said to me. He turned to Scott. "I don't know if I mentioned this before, but Gillian is Ashley's aunt."

"Ashley?" Scott said, appearing momentarily confused. "Oh, yes, Ashley! I work with so many young people, I begin to think of them by their stage names."

"Pastor Jim, could I have just a minute? I have something to tell you," I said, unable to keep the nervousness out of my voice.

"I am at the beck and call of my parishioners night and day," he said, "and if you don't believe me you can just ask my wife." He stopped to chuckle. "But we are up to our elbows right now with this musical and if you could make an appointment for another time, I'd appreciate it."

"This won't take long," I said, "and I wouldn't tell Bob Johanson just yet, but I think we are about to find out exactly who showed up at JoJo's apartment."

Both Pastor Jim and Scott looked at me. "I have no intention of bringing that up to Bob," Pastor Jim said. "He's agitated enough as it is and it can't be doing his health any favors to dwell on JoJo."

That hadn't been the response I was expecting. Pastor Jim was supposed to ask me how we were about to find out.

"Is he that bad off?" Scott asked.

"He certainly doesn't look like he'll be with us much longer, although it'll be up to God to decide when his time here is through."

"Well, someone's time is coming tomorrow night," I said in an effort to get him back on track. "There's a storage unit that Lark rented and I'm going to go through it tomorrow night at about nine or so. JoJo's roommate said she knew who tried to rape her and it's all in a diary in the storage unit." I pulled out a piece of paper with the name of the storage unit and the address and laid it on Pastor Jim's desk.

"Tomorrow night at nine o'clock?" Pastor Jim asked. "Isn't that a little late to be going to Lincoln?"

"Clint and I are going to Lincoln for a foster parent class tomorrow afternoon. Clint's coming back, but I'm going to a storage unit Lark rented."

I moved out into the hall way and Pastor Jim followed me. "You know I'll be in Lincoln tomorrow night, too. It's my evening to lead the Bible study at the Correctional Center. And I'm sorry, I wasn't paying attention, what storage unit of JoJo's are you talking about?"

I hadn't expected Pastor Jim to admit he'd be in Lincoln at the same time, but the question about the storage unit made my heart beat faster. "I left the address on your desk. It's on Van Dorn Street, just east off of Highway 77. Lark rented it after JoJo died to store her personal things. The diary is in there."

"Gillian," Pastor Jim said, "are you asking me to meet you there? I will if you want me to, but I think Lark is wrong. I've talked about this with Bob many times over the years and JoJo didn't know who came to her apartment that night."

"Not right after it happened," I said. "But she figured it out a couple of years later. We'll know who it was when I find that diary tomorrow night."

"And you want me to meet you tomorrow night on Van Dorn Street?" Pastor Jim asked again.

"No, no. I was just telling you so you'd be available for Bob, to counsel him, you know, if he needed it." The nervousness was back in my voice.

Pastor Jim bit at the nail on his little finger. "Sorry," he said noticing that I was watching him. "It's a nervous habit." He put his hand down. "I know Bob wanted you to find this out for him, but I think we all need to ask ourselves what good will come out of giving Bob this information now?"

"He wanted to know," I said.

"Yes, I suppose so." Pastor Jim sighed in resignation. "Was there anything else? Scott and I are supposed to be in the auditorium setting up microphones. One of the teachers in Beatrice loaned them to us and I want the kids to have a chance to use them before the big night."

On Tuesday, after Clint and I finished our class, Clint went to have his fingerprints rolled for the criminal history check that is required for all foster parents. As a probation officer, mine were already on file. I had met Sid at his favorite bakery in south Lincoln and was relaying my conversation and impression of Pastor Jim. The conversation the previous day hadn't gone exactly as Sid had expected, either, and he thought the brush off at the end might be a sign of guilt.

Now it was eight o'clock and I was pulling into the storage complex off of Van Dorn Street, regretting that I had agreed to be part of the trap.

I pulled down a gravel road within the complex and found a blue door with the number 233 painted in black. At least it was one of the small storage units and not a garage, I thought to myself.

Sid was at the nearby Corrections Center and had Pastor Jim's vehicle staked out. I stepped out of my car, went over to the storage unit, and unlocked the door. I stepped into a space the size of a large closet. An antique waterfall dresser and mirror was on one side along with a lamp and a rolled up rug that went nearly to the ceiling. The other side had stacks of clear storage containers which appeared to be full of small, tan boxes.

I propped the door open with one of the containers. I pulled another container down and opened it, inside were small, square boxes that had been covered with cloth and had designs painted on them. I pulled down the next box and opened it. There was a folder with the words Master Bedroom Plan. Inside the folder were the blueprints to all the squares. I looked through the drawings and the pages and saw that each square had a tiny number on the back. The blocks would cover an entire wall and form a garden scene. There would be space between the blocks, but the end result would be a garden scene with a nude Geisha and a tiger. I picked up one of the squares. They were hand painted and the colors were short brush strokes in vivid colors. Someone had spent a lot of time on this. *JoJo had spent a lot of time on this.* This would have been a beautiful. No wonder Lark couldn't bring herself to throw these away.

I also understood now why Lark didn't want Bob to have them either. I'd never been in his house, but I was certain there would be no nude Geishas on the wall. I pulled the next box down and opened it. It was more of the painted squares. On the top of this one, though, were invitations to a barbeque. The invitations had been individually made with a hand painted border and each had a picture of JoJo and a very handsome man. I recognized JoJo immediately. She bore a slight resemblance to Russ in the face, but looked like she could have been in a magazine ad for white teeth and shiny hair. I realized the man in the pictures was Jonathan. He was bronzed and muscular.

From Lark's portrayal, I had envisioned him as weak and sickly. JoJo must have been shocked when she met him for lunch.

Eventually I put the pictures away and stacked the containers back against the wall. I completely understood why Lark had wanted me to throw JoJo's things away; Lark couldn't do it. Well, I couldn't do it, either.

I stepped outside the storage unit and checked my watch: 9:10. A whole hour had passed while I'd been immersed in the artwork and pictures. The bright summer day was already getting hazy and once the sun went down it would be completely dark. My cell phone rang and I jumped.

"Yes," I said.

"Gillian, he's leaving the penitentiary and I'm on his tail. He's heading your way."

"Okay," I breathed the word in the phone.

"What are you doing?" Sid asked.

"I was going through things in the storage unit." I said. "I came outside to get some air." I was sweating and the back of my shirt was sticking to my back.

"Okay, go back into the storage unit. Open something up and start going through it. He'll probably be there in five minutes. I'll stay with him and when he gets there I'll call for backup. We'll wait until he's pretty close to you, then we'll move in and he can do his explaining."

I heard the crunch of my shoes on the gravel as I walked back to the storage unit. I suddenly became very aware of my surroundings. The traffic from Highway 77 was a white noise in the background. Van Dorn Street was not visible because of a stand of trees. The office at the storage complex was visible, but empty. I was completely alone here.

I walked slowly back in the storage unit when the cell phone rang again. The key to the storage unit came out of my pocket along with my cell phone and the key clamored to the floor. "Hello," I said breathlessly.

"A new development," Sid said. "He pulled into a drive-in off of Old Cheney and ordered an ice cream cone. He's sitting in the parking lot eating it."

"Oh," I said.

"I'll call you when he's on the move again. I just wanted to let you know it's going to be longer than I said."

"Okay," I said. I picked the key up and put it back in my pocket. The light switch was on my right and I switched on the overhead bulb. The area wasn't much bigger than a closet and now it felt claustrophobic. I noted the large rug was covered in plastic. I opened the top dresser drawer. Empty.

The dresser mirror reflected the darkness outside and I thought I saw movement. I turned and stepped out of the storage shed and looked up and down the side of the building. A light pole at the end of the building flickered on, triggered by the coming darkness. That was probably the movement I had caught.

I went back inside the storage unit and turned my attention to the dresser. I opened the middle drawer. There was a note. In shaky handwriting reminiscent of Bob Johanson's, someone had written, *this dresser belonged to Becky's grandmother*. Bob wouldn't have referred to his daughter as Becky, it must be Jonathan's handwriting. I put the note back in the drawer and closed it.

The hair on the back of my neck stood up. I looked out into the falling blackness and knew with certainty that someone was watching me. My cell phone rang and with trembling hands I pulled it out of my pocket.

"Gillian?" Sid's voice was a relief to hear.

"Are you here?" I whispered.

"No. He finished his ice cream and now he's turning south on Highway 77 toward Bend Brook. It looks like he's going home."

"Sid," the word came out in a rasp.

"What?" I could hear the change in his voice.

"I'm not," I paused and looked out into the darkness, "I'm not alone."

"Who's with you?"

"I don't know. I can't see anyone, I just know somebody's watching me."

"Are you sure?"

"Yes," I stammered.

"Where are you?"

"In the storage unit."

"Listen to me carefully and do exactly what I say. Leave now. Go to your car and get in. Lock the doors and drive away. I'm hanging up and calling for backup." I looked at the cell and it said the call had ended. I looked out at the darkness and my car parked on the other side of the road. I'd go to the car, lock myself in, and then I'd drive to the entrance and wait for Sid.

I walked out of the storage unit leaving the light on and the door open. I dug in my pocket for my car keys. I got the car keys out and dropped the storage key. I picked it up and walked toward the car. There was movement on the other side of my car. A ski-masked face looked back at me through the passenger window. I screamed, dropped the keys and ran back toward the storage shed.

I kicked the container that was holding the door open and hurtled into the storage unit. Gasping for air, I reached for my pocket. My cell phone had been in my hand with the keys. The keys! The key to the storage unit was outside. I looked around for a weapon and grabbed the rug. I pulled it and it fell toward the door, hitting the light bulb in the process and throwing me into total darkness. I grabbed hold of the rug and sobbed.

I heard a key in the storage unit lock. The lock clicked and I saw a slice of light and a gloved hand on the door frame. I lurched forward to pull the door shut. The gloved hand caught in the door frame and there was a yelp of pain.

The doorknob was wrenched from my grip and pulled open. I grabbed the top storage tub and pulled it down while the person lunged into the storage shed, trying to maneuver past the rug. I pulled the other storage boxes down, tripped and fell backwards into the wall.

Hands grabbed my leg and started to pull. I screamed and grabbed hold of one of the dresser legs. Suddenly the hands went limp. I jerked my leg free and crawled to the side of the dresser where the rug had been. I heard the faint wail of a siren. It was coming closer.

There was crunching noise of gravel as my assailant ran down the roadway. I stood up, leaned against the dresser and tried to breathe.

I had scraped both my knees on the cement floor although I hadn't felt it at the time. After giving a statement to the responding police officer, I now sat in the back of a police cruiser, picking bits of light bulb out of my knees with tweezers. Sid sat beside me, writing in a notebook and occasionally talking on his cell phone.

An LPD officer came over to the window and spoke to Sid. "Somebody tried to booby trap her car."

"Is it safe to drive?" I asked.

"We're still checking, but we think so. He left all his car tools here," the officer said. "They're quality tools," he added.

"Stolen?" Sid asked.

The officer shrugged. "Hard to say."

Sid turned to me, "you did good, kid."

"It's too bad the bait idea didn't work," I said. "Because I have no intention of ever doing it again!"

"What do you mean it didn't work?" Sid asked. "It worked. We were just watching the wrong fish."

TWENTY

After Tuesday night, I wanted a calm Wednesday. What I wanted and what I got were two different things. Clint was furious about the previous night. He was even more angry when my cell phone rang in the middle of our conversation. I saw it was Sid's number and answered.

"Sid," I said. "Did they catch him?"

"Not that I know of, I just called to see if you've seen the Lincoln paper. The other fish is in it."

"The other fish?" I asked.

"Yep, the Montgomery family donated an organ to one of the churches in Lincoln. They had a program for the public last night and guess who's wheeling his wife into church?"

"Scott?" I said.

"Yep," Sid said. "My other fish."

"What are you going to do now?"

"I'm going back to the drawing board to see if I missed anything," Sid said.

I disconnected the call and turned my attention back to Clint. He was standing by the kitchen counter, pouring a cup of coffee. "I thought Sid was going to be right behind you the whole time," he said.

"I did, too," I said, "but that's just not how it worked out." I finished buttering a slice of toast at the kitchen table and considered offering it to Clint.

"What kind of cop is he anyway, to set something like that up?" Clint sat down at the table.

"He said he had a hunch and needed to test it," I said.

"I hope you are going to drop this whole thing," he said.

"Don't worry, I told Sid I'm not going to be bait again," I said. "And besides, there are other things I need to concentrate on."

Clint gave me a skeptical look. "Such as?" he asked.

"I think Josh might be right about Jessica not being Logan's mother. She's so petite, I don't know how she could have hidden a full-term pregnancy."

"Does it matter?" Clint sighed. "From what you've said, it doesn't sound like she has any intention of putting Logan up for adoption. I know we had our hearts set on Logan, but I think it's time to move on and apply to some of the adoption agencies."

"You're right," I said, "she'll never give up Logan. It's just that I think Jessica's hiding something. I want to talk to the doctor at the hospital and see just who he examined. If Jessica is raising someone else's baby, I need to know."

"I guess that might not be a bad idea."

"Could you get a copy of last year's high school annual from Josh?" I asked.

"If Josh will give it up," Clint said. "But what good will that do?"

"I'm going to show it to the doctor who was on duty when Jessica and Logan were brought in. If Jessica was the girl he examined, I'd think he'd remember her and would be able to identify her as Logan's birth mother."

"I think maybe both you and Josh are watching too much CSI." He got up and dumped the rest of his coffee in the sink. "I'd better be going if I'm going to be back here by one o'clock.

"Do you think the house looks okay?" I asked.

Clint shrugged. "I flipped the couch cushions so you can't see where Coco chewed."

I was at work when Marlene called. A call from Marlene is not normally a bad thing, but this was to remind me about Friday night. Again. "Don't forget we are having a dessert bar afterwards. It would be nice if you could bring something special."

"I already have my dessert planned," I said.

"Oh, good! That was a nice looking chocolate torte your mother made last Saturday, even though we didn't stay to eat any of it."

"I'm not bringing a chocolate torte," I said.

"Lemon bars? Your lemon bars are very good."

"Ummm, not lemon bars," I said. "but you're getting closer."

"Tell me!" Marlene said.

"Danish," I said.

"Grocery store Danish?" she said, her voice flat.

"No, this is bakery Danish. They're very good."

"Well, okay," she sighed. "Be at the hall by 6:30. Don't forget!"

"I won't, but I've got to go. I have an appointment," I said.

At least I thought I had an appointment. Arnold Taylor was on probation for a DUI and the reason he wasn't at his appointment was because he had been cited for DUI. Again. He was currently in the Fairbury jail. Once I realized he wasn't going to show, I decided I should go home and dust the house. Before I was out the door, though, the judge dropped off paperwork for a pre-sentence investigation. As a result, I made it home just in time for the home visit from Health and Human Services. A thin woman with teased hair carefully poked and prodded through our house while we stood back and watched. At the end of the visit, she gave us a list of things we needed to change around the house.

"Your top priority," she said, "is to childproof everything. You've got cleansers and other poisons under the sinks in the kitchen and the bathroom. You've got electric sockets that need childproof covers, and that door to the stairs has to stay shut. It's all in the list here."

I took the proffered list.

"That's it?" Clint said.

"One more thing," she said. "The dog out in the yard? It's not a breed that would pose a threat to a child, is it?"

"Coco is a chocolate Lab, they're a hunting breed but she's too timid to hunt," Clint said.

"She's completely harmless," I said.

"The worse she'll do is drool on you," Clint said. "Come see for yourself."

We went outside. "Coco," Clint called. Coco shot up the porch steps to Clint. "Sit, girl, sit," he said, pushing Coco down.

See how friendly she is?" I said. "She wouldn't hurt a fly."

The woman reached out to pet Coco, and Coco snapped at her, knicking her finger.

"I just did not see that coming," Clint said.

We were both sitting on the couch, Coco at our feet, contentedly chewing on a rawhide bone.

"We should have had Coco around her a little longer before we said anything. Coco doesn't see a lot of strangers," I said.

"Yeah, but she's never bitten anyone before."

"It wasn't really a bite," I said. "And at least we had Band-Aids and peroxide on hand. Maybe she'll give us points for that," I said.

"I doubt it," Clint said. "She didn't seem all that nice."

"How could you tell if she was nice or not?" I asked. "We just met her."

"Nice or not, I just didn't like her," Clint said.

"Why not?" I asked.

"She made it sound like any kid that came into this house might never get out alive with all the poison and unsafe stairs and outlets," Clint said.

"It's just her job," I said. "You know what? I bet Coco sensed you didn't like her and that's why she snapped at her."

We looked at Coco who noticed the attention and thumped her tail against the floor.

My cell phone rang. I looked at the number and wrinkled my nose. "It's Dot," I said. "Yes?"

"Gillian, is your home visit over with because we have a situation developing here."

"What kind of situation?" I asked.

"There's a woman who's called just about every number in this courthouse looking for a female probation officer. She doesn't have your name, but she wants your home number. Do you know who she is?"

"That could be anybody," I said.

"I know," Dot agreed. "I didn't think I should give her your name or home number, though, unless you want me to?"

The last part of the sentence was said hopefully. "No, Dot, give her my office phone and tell her I'll be there in ten minutes."

I was back at the courthouse in five minutes. The caller was holding on Judy's line and Dot was directing phone traffic. "Get in your office, Gillian."

"I'm on my way," I said, unlocking the door.

"Judy, transfer her in," Dot said.

My phone rang.

"State Probation Office," I said.

"Are you the probation officer I met last week?" a husky female voice demanded.

"I don't know," I said, turning on my computer and trying to place the voice. "What's your name?"

"LaShawn Devoe. A probation officer came to my home . . ."

"That was me," I interrupted. "I came to see Lark McCallister."

"You!" she yelled into the phone and I held it away from my ear. "You need to help me! Lark is missing and the police won't do anything about it. I'm at LaGuardia waiting for a plane, I didn't plan on leaving this early so I'm on standby . . ."

"Wait," I said. "If you're in New York, how do you know Lark's missing?"

"She didn't call me! She calls me everyday and she didn't call. I tried calling her cell and I finally called her work and one of the girls went over to check on her a little bit ago and she's not there. She said the morning paper is there and there's a notice about the lawn maintenance stuck in the door, but Lark's gone and it doesn't look like she came home last night."

"Maybe she went somewhere else for the night." I said.

"No!" I held the phone further away from my ear. "She wouldn't have gone anywhere else. Plus she's not answering her cell phone! One of the other girls she works with called me a little bit ago after she heard Lark was missing. She said Lark had plans to meet someone after work last night and I know it was someone who was involved in that JoJo thing that you were talking . . ."

"Wait," I said. "Have you told this to the police?"

"I already told you, the police won't do anything! First they said it hasn't been forty-eight hours and then when they found out where she worked, they said someone would get back to me in a couple of days!"

"Hold on," I said. "Why are you're calling me about this?"

"Because this is your fault! She was meeting someone because you came and talked to her and got her all upset about JoJo! I want you to go to the police station in Omaha and make them file a missing person report. And then I want you to go find her!"

TWENTY-ONE

My phone call to the Omaha Police Department had resulted in a promise that an officer would call me within the next thirty-six hours. In desperation, I had called Sid who was more than happy to accompany me to the Omaha Police Department. He was also more than happy to grill me about the phone call from LaShawn.

"So," Sid began for the umpteenth time, "Lark went missing Tuesday night, that's what her girlfriend said, right?"

"I don't think she said 'Tuesday night' specifically," I said.

"But that's the night Lark didn't show up for work, right?" Sid persisted.

"Yes, wait, I mean no. LaShawn said it was last night, Wednesday night, that she didn't show up for work. It was Tuesday night that she was supposed to meet someone."

"Humph," Sid said.

"What's the matter?" I asked, looking over at him.

"Well, for one thing, you're not watching the road."

I swung my head and my attention back to the road, ever mindful of how fast an accident can happen.

"That's better," Sid said. "Now, the other thing that I'm having problems with here is who was at the storage unit if Lark made arrangements to meet our guy the same night?"

"LaShawn said Lark was meeting someone after she got off work on Tuesday. Her Tuesday night would be our Wednesday morning," I said.

"Well, what does this guy do, take Geritol? Okay, here's the next thing that bothers me. You said in your statement that the guy tried to pull you out of the storage unit."

"He grabbed my leg" I said. "I think he was going to pull me out, but I don't know. Remember I was upset that night."

"Yeah, but that's just not like my guy. He didn't fight with his victims."

"He was desperate," I said. "He would have wanted to get rid of me."

"And you said you shut the door on his hand?"

"I felt the door crunch his hand," I said. "And he yelled."

"I checked all the hospitals to see if any hand injuries were reported, but nothing panned out."

I looked over at Sid. "Do you think I'm exaggerating? I'm not."

"Watch the road! We're on the interstate, for crying out loud. And no, I don't think you're exaggerating. I just think maybe someone else showed up at the storage unit."

"Someone else? What do you mean someone else?" I glanced at Sid.

"Maybe we didn't catch anyone in our net Tuesday night. Maybe you were just in the wrong place at the wrong time."

"He planned it," I said. "He had tools to jimmy my car."

"Or he had tools to break into the storage units," Sid said. "It's an isolated area and I wouldn't be surprised if some of the larger units had cars in them."

"And then he saw me and just decided to attack? Why would he do that?" I asked.

"He's a criminal. Some specialize, some don't," Sid said. "I just don't know if he's the criminal we're looking for." Sid undid his seat belt and reached into his pant pocket. He pulled out a cigar and put his seatbelt back on.

"Hey! You aren't smoking in my car," I said.

"I am not smoking," he said, biting a piece of the cellophane wrapper off. "I am thinking and this helps me think."

Sid now sat on a bench in a hallway of the Omaha Police Department chewing on his cigar. I sat down by him.

A uniformed officer walked by and gave Sid a dirty look. "I'm chewing, not smoking," Sid growled. "Well?" he asked, looking back at me.

"It's useless," I said. "I talked to a detective who said a report has been turned in but they aren't going to open an investigation because they have no indication of foul play."

"And?"

I took some Kleenex out of my purse. "And nothing! We might as well go home. He won't listen. He said she's an adult and it's not up to them to monitor her movements."

Sid took the cigar out of his mouth. "Gillian, I'm going to say something you don't generally hear from a policeman, retired or otherwise, but here it goes: For every good cop out there, there's a not-so-good cop."

"You think I've got a bad cop?" I asked.

"I don't know. Let me take a look at this guy, and then I'll tell you what I think," Sid said.

I glanced at Sid to see if he was serious.

Sid stood up. "Which desk?" he asked.

"There's two guys in the front and he's the one on the right," I said.

Sid walked down the hallway and looked into the area I had just left. He put the cigar in his mouth and chewed a little before coming back down the hall and sitting down by me. "He's not a bad cop" Sid said.

"He's not?" I repeated.

"No," Sid said. "He's just a dumb schmuck. He doesn't get it."

"How can he not get it?" I asked.

"Let me tell you a little story." He slouched back and crossed one leg over the other. "Back in the mid-70's, I became a sergeant in the domestic and sexual assault unit. It was all lumped together. Anyway, this guy, Tony, transferred in and he wasn't good for our unit. He was changing things, and it wasn't a good change. But the guys in our unit, they just loved him."

"The women, too?"

"Ha! Didn't have any women then, just men. Well, we had some matrons and meter maids, but when we went out on calls, it was just men. That was the way it was in those days."

"But he wasn't a good guy?"

"Oh, he was a great guy. He told funny stories, he was a good looking kid, too, except his nose was crooked. He was an ex-boxer, and this was right when those Rocky movies started coming out so the other guys would ask him questions about boxing and he'd brag that he'd gotten his nose broke four times."

I shrugged. "Sounds like a likeable guy."

"Oh, he was, all right."

"What was the problem, then?"

"It was his sense of humor. Not that I don't have a good sense of humor, but Tony's sense of humor was at the expense of the people he was supposed to be helping."

"You're kidding? He'd joke with rape victims?"

"No, not exactly with them. And you have to keep in mind, Gillian, we did the domestics and rapes, and it could be very frustrating. We had a woman named DeeDee whose husband beat her up just about every first and third Fridays because those were his paydays. He'd get drunk, come home and hit her and she'd call us when things got too ugly. We'd usually try and keep an officer on reserve for those days. We called it DeeDee duty. It was cop humor."

"How sad."

"Yeah. Very sad. She never wanted to press charges, and as far as I know she never left him. In today's world, she wouldn't have any say about the charges. But anyway, back to Tony. He started making a joke out of the cases he worked on and the newer cops were beginning to follow suit. He knew I didn't think he was funny, so he started pointing out mistakes I made."

"So you'd look like the bad guy, so to speak."

Sid nodded. "You got it. Anyway, one night I go to the bar with Tony and two of the newer recruits. This time he's yukking it up, telling us how this woman wants her ex-boyfriend charged with rape. He asked if their relationship had been sexual when they were still together and she'd said yes. Then he'd asked her how many times she had sex with her ex-boyfriend and the woman started to count. She'd marked it on her calendar."

"Maybe she was trying not to get pregnant."

"Maybe. But she found her calendar and gave Tony an exact number. Tony's punch line at the bar that night was that it wasn't a rape, it was the fifty-ninth time she'd had sex with the guy that year. Then he put his head back and laughed and the other guys laughed, too."

"What a jerk. I hope you fired him."

"Nope." Sid shook his head. "I laughed right along with them. Then, later when we're all leaving, we walk to the parking lot out back and the four of us are the only ones out in the lot. Tony is heading toward his car and I said 'Hey, Tony, come over here' and he did. Well, let me tell you, you can't grow up in the neighborhood I grew up in and not know something about boxing. I pulled my arm back and hit him in the nose straight up. I maybe hit him a little too hard because it knocked him down and there was blood gushing all over the front of his shirt. My knuckles were zinging with pain and I'm thinking I must have broke my hand but I just smiled like nothing's the matter. Tony starts to get up, and he's telling me I'm a stupid moron, or you know, words to that effect."

"He must have been furious," I said.

Sid waved the cigar around. "Yeah, yeah, he was, but it was sort of hard to understand him. Anyway, I think he's going to come for me and I'm getting a little scared. The other guys are holding him back."

"Sid, you hit him. What were you thinking?" I asked.

"That's pretty much what one of the other guys said so I said 'is there a problem?' and Tony said there was one hell of a problem, that I'd just assaulted him and I was going to pay for it."

"Well, I just stood there and shrugged. 'It shouldn't matter,' I said. The new guys just looked at me with open mouths and one of them said, 'Sarge, what in the hell do you mean it shouldn't matter? That was aggravated assault,'

So I said, 'No, it wasn't. It was just the fifth time he broke his nose.' And I put my head back and laughed."

"What did they say?"

"Nothing. None of them said a damn thing. I said, 'well, that's funny ain't it?' and they still didn't say nothing. We just stood in that parking lot and listened to the wind chase some leaves around the pavement. Then I tipped my hat to them with the hand I could still use and said 'I'll see you guys at work.' I got in my car, thinking how in the hell am I going to drive, because by that time I couldn't close my fist. When I got home, Delores packed my hand in ice and she said 'you fool, you're going to lose your job.'"

"Did you?"

"No, although I wasn't so sure about it that night. I didn't sleep at all, I was so worried that I'd be fired."

"What happened?" I asked.

"Well, the next day I went to shift change and everybody's quiet and I knew the word had gone around and everybody in that room knew about me and Tony. So I figure I'm going to give it to them straight. I gave them the same spiel I give everybody when they start the unit. I told them the women we deal with are someone's daughter or sister or mother and they are to be treated like you'd want your daughter or sister or mother to be treated. Then I looked around the room and said 'I won't tolerate anything less.' Nowadays they have all sorts of training crap you go through, but not back then."

"What did they say?"

"Nothing." Sid's teeth clenched the cigar.

"Maybe they didn't know you punched Tony," I said.

"Oh, they knew. Everybody knew. It was just never brought up again."

"What happened to Tony?"

"He got it. He still made jokes, you got to, but he understood there was a line and he didn't cross it again."

"And he never filed a complaint against you?"

"No, but he did eventually transfer to homicide."

I sat back and put the Kleenex back in my purse. "Sid, you go tell that officer about Lark. He'll listen to you."

"He might. But," Sid dragged the last word out, "he'd probably think I'm sticking my nose where it don't belong. And is he going to change his way of thinking if I pull rank on him?"

"Maybe," I said.

"Did you listen to the story I just told you?" Sid asked. "That dumb schmuck in there doesn't get it. He hears the word 'exotic dancer' and he thinks Lark is some stripper who took off with some john. He doesn't see her as a victim and he won't unless you go in there and tell him different. Tell him about her stocks, about LaShawn. He won't get it unless you make him understand." Sid's thin lips curled around the cigar.

I stared at the blank wall across from me and then I looked at Sid. "Okay," I said. "But why did you even come with me if you were just going to sit out here in the hall?"

He took the cigar out of his mouth. "I came to sit in your corner. And give you a push back in the ring if you needed it."

I walked back down the hall and into the room. "Sgt. Davidson," I said. "I have more information on Lark McCallister."

TWENTY-TWO

Clint had left Josh's yearbook on the dining room table. I flipped through the book and found Jessica's picture. Her lips were turned up in a small smile, making her chin seem a little more pointed. There was a hollow at the base of her neck and her collar bones protruded from either side. She didn't have an ounce of fat on her, how could she have hidden a pregnancy?

I called the Beatrice Hospital to find out who had been the doctor on duty in the emergency room the day Logan was born. After locating that information and a phone number for Dr. William Schneider, I left messages at the hospital and his office. He returned the call and we agreed to meet in the hospital cafeteria the next day at ten o'clock. He said he'd be there after he finished his rounds.

Friday morning I called into the courthouse and left a message with the judge and Dot that I would be available by cell phone.

"I work until five so I should have plenty of time to get ready for the musical," Clint said as I was leaving.

I stopped and turned back to Clint. "I should be back before then. We'll bring the Danish in the fridge for the dessert bar."

"Oh," Clint said. "I just had two of them."

"Don't eat anymore! That's what we are bringing for the dessert bar after the musical." I left the house wondering if I was starting to sound like Marlene. I drove to the hospital and had ample time to ponder what it would take to be Marlene while I sipped exceedingly strong and bitter iced tea and waited for Dr. Schneider. It was nearly eleven o'clock when a tall, big-boned man with a wide face and high forehead walked into the cafeteria, scanned the tables while he paid for his iced tea, and then walked over to me.

"Dr. Schneider?" I asked.

"Yes," he answered, sitting down across from me.

"Thanks for meeting with me," I said.

"I only have a few minutes," he replied curtly.

So much for an apology for his lateness. "This shouldn't take long," I said. "I need to talk to the doctor who examined a girl who had a baby at home. This would have been nearly two years ago . . ."

"I'm that doctor," he said.

"You're sure?" I asked.

"Quite," he said.

"I just want you to identify the patient you had at the emergency room." I opened the year book to the page with Jessica's picture.

"I can't help you there," he said.

"Just take a look," I said, holding the book out. "I know it was two years ago, but you might remember."

"Oh, I remember perfectly well, but I can't give out medical information unless you have a signed HIPPA consent form from the patient."

"She's under eighteen," I said, "and I'm her probation officer."

"Then a signed form from the parent slash guardian." He picked up a pink packet of sugar and thwacked it three times with his thumb and index finger with such force and precision that had it been alive, I'm sure it would have responded.

I laid the book down on the table. "Let me explain," I said. "I'm not asking for medical information. I just want clarification. I'm the probation officer for the girl who's been charged with leaving her newborn baby under a bridge. I think it might be somebody else's child and she just took the baby and claimed it as hers."

"Ahhh!" he said, pouring the sugar into his iced tea. "You want me to identify your client."

"Yes," I said, relieved that he'd taken an interest in the subject. "I know . . ." I didn't get to finish my sentence because his thumb and forefinger had thwacked on the open annual.

"Top row, second to the right. That's your client," he said.

"Yes," I said. "It is." So much for that theory.

He stirred his tea and pursed his lips. "She shouldn't be on probation for leaving a baby under a bridge."

"Technically, she's on probation for child endangerment," I said

He shrugged, and took another drink of tea.

"Why did you say she shouldn't be on probation for leaving the baby under a bridge?"

"Again, I can't speak to her medical condition," he said.

"Okay," I said, shutting the book. "What can you tell me?"

"Absolutely nothing about your client. But I can speak in generalities. Shall we do that?"

"Fine," I said.

"Did you know that childbirth is the leading cause of death and disability for women of reproductive age?" he asked.

Oh, great. I was going to get a lecture. "I don't know of anyone who's died in childbirth."

"Of course you don't. Here in the United States everyone has access to medical facilities. Unfortunately, that can't be said of other countries in the world and I was speaking of all countries, not just the United States." He stirred his tea, apparently deep in thought. "Let's stop with the generalities for a minute and let me suggest something," he said. "I think it will help you."

"I'm open to suggestions," I said.

"You should obtain a copy of the police report."

"I do have a copy of the report in her file," I said

"And what does that report say about the medical condition of your client?" he asked.

I thought back to the report. "It doesn't really tell me anything about her medical condition. I think the report said she was transported to the hospital." I said.

"Then perhaps you should obtain more information from the police officer," he suggested.

I fidgeted. "It was the sheriff who handled the case and I'm not on the best terms with him right now."

He sipped his iced tea and frowned. "But he told you that your client left the baby under the bridge?"

"I can't remember if I was told that specifically but that's the impression that was given at the time."

"Haven't you talked to her about this?" he asked. "You're her probation officer, after all."

I winced. "That's just it. She isn't very forthcoming about the situation. I thought she might have been covering for a friend, which would raise issues not only with the charge against her but with custody of the child. That's why I wanted you to identify her so I would know for sure."

He inhaled deeply through his nose, the way people do before they attempt a difficult task. "Again, I'd like to remind you I'm speaking in general terms of childbirth. Have you heard the old wives tales about the women who gave birth in the field and went home to make dinner for the family?"

"Yes," I said.

"And perhaps you've heard about the prom attendee who went into the bathroom and had a baby before she danced to the last song of the night?"

I nodded. "I think I read about that a couple of years ago."

"Please don't misunderstand." He smiled briefly. "I'm certainly not saying there aren't some very hardy women who delivered their babies and then went about their daily routines, but in reality, births without medical assistance have a much higher rate of mortality for both the child and the mother. As I stated before, childbirth is the leading cause of death and disability for women of reproductive age. A hundred years ago it wasn't the least bit uncommon to lose both the mother and infant during childbirth."

He took a drink of his tea and studied me across the Formica with intense blue eyes. "Do you," he began slowly, "want to hear about one of the most common complications?"

I nodded, with dawning realization that what he was going to tell me was relevant to Jessica. "Yes," I said, "I want to hear about one of the most common complications."

"It's excessive bleeding. This can be a result of several things, for instance a tear in the uterine lining will cause bleeding, especially if the mother was carrying a large baby. Bleeding also results if the entire placenta is not delivered."

"The doctor always checks the placenta after the baby is born," I said.

He nodded. "A doctor will check the placenta to make sure it's complete and none is left in the uterus. If part of the placenta is left in the uterus, it may cause excessive bleeding. Now, there is always lochia, or bleeding, after delivery but if even a small fragment of the placenta remained in the uterus, blood would flow through the placenta via open blood vessels in the uterus, meaning the patient would be hemorrhaging."

He stared at me intensely again.

"How long," I asked, "would the patient have before she knew she was hemorrhaging?"

He shrugged. "That would depend on the circumstances. And the heavy bleeding might not start right away, but in most cases it does. At first, the woman might feel dizzy or faint when she stood up and moved around. Then her pulse would increase and her blood pressure would drop and eventually she would go into shock. Death would follow unless, of course, she was given a blood transfusion and the placenta was removed, either by a D & C or a hysterectomy."

I took a sip of my iced tea, while I formed my next question. "In a situation like that, is there a way the woman could postpone the heavy bleeding or try to stop it herself?"

His eyebrows lifted. "Well, I have seen patients with bathroom towels packed between their legs in an effort to stop the bleeding on their own."

"Have you," I paused, "seen a patient with towels packed between her legs in the last two years?" I was beginning to feel a numb cold either from the air conditioning or our conversation.

"As a matter of fact, I have." He drained his iced tea and rattled the ice. "And it is these common complications of childbirth which preclude some women from returning to field work or making dinner for their family."

"Or," I said quietly, "running around in ditches."

He nodded over the empty glass. "That, too," he said.

I was now both cold and queasy. "I realize you're limited in what you can say by the privacy laws, but I wish you had found a way to convey this information to someone sooner." I said.

"Oh, but I did!" He shook a piece of ice out of the glass and into his mouth. "And I didn't have to find anyone. They came to me."

"Who came to you?" I asked.

He crunched the ice in his mouth. "A law enforcement officer whose name escapes me at the moment, and your former county attorney, Wendell Krackenberg."

TWENTY-THREE

I drove slowly down the streets of downtown Beatrice, Nebraska. Wendell Krackenberg had moved his practice and personal residence to Beatrice after losing the county attorney position to Trent Green. I didn't have an exact address for Wendell's office, but I knew the approximate location.

It was shortly before one o'clock and I hoped he wasn't at lunch – or out of the office altogether. I stopped abruptly when I saw a window with Krackenberg Law Office in white letters. Then better luck – I recognized Wendell's lumbering gait, he was walking down the opposite side of the street. I did a U-turn and pulled into an open parking space.

"Gillian!" Wendell said as I got out of the car, "aren't you a sight for sore eyes!"

"Wendell," I acknowledged the big bear of a man with the thatch of brown hair. He offered a hand and pumped my hand enthusiastically. Under his other arm was a legal pad and a sheaf of papers. "Are you going to the courthouse?" I asked.

"No," he shook his head. "Court ran long this morning, I was just coming back to drop these papers at my office and grab a bite of lunch. Have you eaten yet?"

My stomach growled in response. I hadn't eaten breakfast yet, either. "No, I haven't, but I was hoping to talk to you in private, maybe we could go to your office?"

"The café down the street is just as good. And they've got a darned good chicken salad sandwich."

The lunch crowd was still in evidence, but Wendell and I found a table in the corner. It was near the bathrooms, but otherwise secluded. A young girl gave us ice water while a waitress with a tray of dirty dishes stood behind her. "You want your usual?" the waitress said to Wendell.

"You know I do," Wendell said.

"How about you, hon?" she looked at me.

"She'd probably like to see a menu," Wendell said.

"Actually, I'll have the same," I said.

"The very same?" she asked.

"Yes," I said.

"Okay, then," she rebalanced the tray and hustled away.

"So, what brings you to Beatrice?" Wendell asked, taking a sip of the water.

"Jessica Coffers," I replied.

Wendell made a face over his water glass. "You know, that's one memory lane I don't want to stroll down."

"I was just at the hospital; I talked to Dr. Schneider. He said you talked to him, too. You must have known things weren't adding up," I said.

Wendell blotted his lips with his napkin. "Oh, I knew things weren't adding up, all right. Newt's reports on the Coffer's incident were shoddy and vague. Of course, Newt's wife and Steve's sister, Ginny, are first cousins. Plus Newt and Mitch have been friends for as long as I can remember."

"Why didn't you do something?" I asked. "Newt had to have known Jessica didn't have the stamina to get to the bridge after she gave birth, yet he treats her like she's America's Most Wanted."

"You just hit part of the nail on the head. No one was cooperating, not Newt, not Jessica, not Mitch, no one. It makes it dammed hard to file charges when things don't make sense and no one will talk."

"But you did file a charge of child endangerment against Jessica," I reminded him.

"I think it's safe to say she told absolutely no one she was pregnant and, by doing so, she had an unassisted birth and put the baby's life in danger. Consequently, I filed the child endangerment charge." He looked sternly across the table at me. "I said it then and I'll say it now: It was the only charge warranted."

"But Jessica didn't get to that bridge without help. Why didn't you say something?" I asked.

"I didn't get the chance! As I said before, I couldn't get anyone to cooperate. I did get Jessica to commit to a 'no, sir,' when I asked if she had told anyone about her pregnancy and a 'yes, sir' when I asked if she wanted to keep the baby. So I filed the appropriate charge and planned on filing more charges when I had the complete picture. I never got to that point. The whole thing just blew up in my face. Newspaper reporters didn't just call me, they showed up on my doorstep! I couldn't answer the phone without some crackpot lecturing me. Hell, I couldn't walk down the street in Bend Brook without Trudy March verbally accosting me." He stopped talking as the waitress put down sandwiches with chips and glasses of ice tea. A huge amount of pickles garnished each plate.

"I forgot to tell you I always order extra pickles," Wendell said, opening his sandwich and adding some of the pickles.

"Do you want some of mine?" I asked.

"Maybe," he said, glancing at my plate. "Anyway, I stopped talking, too, because anything I said at that point was being misconstrued. If you'll remember, when I said we needed a thorough investigation everyone jumped to the conclusion that I hadn't thought it through when I filed the child endangerment charge. Now, if I had been specific and said Newt needed more in his report, people would have thought I was using Newt as a scapegoat. It was a no-win situation." Wendell took a bite of his sandwich, chewed and swallowed. He looked across at my plate. "You aren't eating anything." he said.

My sandwich and ice tea sat untouched in front of me. "It's too bad Trent Green didn't talk to you about this. The last time I saw Trent, Trudy was pushing him to file charges against Jessica."

Wendell picked up a pickle and put it in his mouth. "Really? Well, I guess that isn't too surprising. Trudy did lead the pack to elect Trent."

"She contributed money, too," I said. "I think Trent promised he'd file new charges in exchange for the campaign contribution."

"Well, if Trent had looked at my trial file, he could have picked up where I left off. I think a review of that file would have shut Trudy up for good. And," he wagged a pickle at me, "Doris would have told him where to find that file. It's in the storage room."

I shifted in my seat. "What do you mean trial file? There's a lot of files in your storage room. They couldn't have all gone to trial."

"You just figured out my trick," Wendell smiled. "Whether I go to trial or not, I keep everything, and I mean everything. Pleadings, reports, statements, you name it. People think I have a good memory but truth be told, I just keep track of things."

I thought back to the time when everything had been in the paper. "Besides the medical information, would there have been anything else in the file that would have helped Trent with Trudy March?" I asked.

Wendell chuckled. "You always cut to the chase, don't you? Now, before I go further, I want you to understand that nothing has been proven. I really wanted Jessica to go to trial. In fact, I begged her to go to trial. Had she done that, I would have been able to call witnesses and request tests, but she was adamant about pleading and she was absolutely distressed when I said there were other places she could stay beside the Banners."

"But Wendell," I said, "so what if Trent knew you wanted Jessica to go to trial rather than plead?"

"Oh, but Trent would have seen my personal notes, my strategy," he took a bite of his sandwich and chewed. "There would have been a list of things that I would have done if we had been going to trial."

"And that would be?" I asked.

"Well, first I would have asked Newt to recuse himself for personal reasons," Wendell said, "and then I would have ordered a paternity test for Mitch Banner."

TWENTY-FOUR

My heart raced as I drove along the two lane highway between Beatrice and Bend Brook. I watched the blue and yellow wildflowers in the ditch go by in a blur. After a car had crossed the center line on Highway 6 and shattered my ankle as well as my first marriage, I had lost faith in the protective abilities of dotted yellow lines. Afterward there were times when a car coming toward me on a highway would cause me to panic. Today was different, my heart was fluttering and my hands were sweating as I gripped the wheel, but I didn't feel panic.

As I neared Bend Brook and reached a sign that warned me to reduce my speed, I felt a sudden sense of purpose. I knew what I had to do.

I pulled up to the courthouse and parked adjacent to the Sheriff's car. Good, I thought, Newt was in his office. Inside the courthouse, I went up the steps and through the glass door which led to the second floor offices.

Dot was standing behind the counter. "Goodness, I thought it was Friday afternoon," she said pointedly. "Oh, it is, I was momentarily confused when I saw you here."

I ignored her, got my keys out, went into my office and shut the door. The red light on my phone was blinking. I punched in the numbers to hear the messages. The first one was the click of a phone hanging up. The second message was the same. On the the third message, there was a pause before the caller identified himself as Bob Johanson, "Call me when you can."

I cringed. I hadn't told Bob anything. Yet. Another conversation I didn't want to have. I flipped through my rolodex, wiped the sweat off of my brow and dialed. Kay answered the phone.

"May I speak to Jessica, please," I asked.

"Hello," Jessica's quiet voice came on the line.

"This is Gillian Jones. I need you to come to my office in the courthouse," I said.

"Now?" she asked.

"Yes, now," I said.

"Is this for a random drug test?"

Good answer! an announcer in my head responded amidst a round of applause. I closed my eyes. "Yes," I said. "It's a random drug test."

"Just a minute and let me see if Kay will watch Logan," Jessica said.

"No!" I said a little too forcefully. "I need to see Logan, too."

"Logan, too?" she echoed.

"Just a standard check," I said. "To make sure that he's okay."

"Oh," she answered.

"How soon can you be here?" I asked. She covered the phone and I heard distorted voices in the background.

"Half an hour?" she asked.

"I'll see you in half an hour," I said.

I pulled Jessica's file from my cabinet drawer and looked through it. I glanced at the clock. It would be another fifteen minutes before Jessica arrived. I left my office with the file, went down the steps, past the front entrance and took the steps to the basement where the Sherriff's Department was housed. Newt looked up from his desk when I walked through the door. He had been flipping through a law enforcement magazine.

He watched me with depthless blue eyes.

"Who," I said calmly, "is your primary suspect in the Trent Green murder?"

"Jessica Coffers," he said, just as evenly.

"And she would want Trent Green dead because . . ." I tilted my hand toward him in a gesture that indicated he should answer.

"I'm not playing your little games." He turned his attention back to the magazine in front of him.

"Let's see, when I look at your report," I flipped through the file to one of the back pages, "I see you summed up her crime with 'Sheriff Newton made contact with Mitch Banner and Jessica Coffers and confirmed that Jessica Coffers had given birth. The baby and Coffers were at the bridge which crossed the road between property owned by the Banners and the Lohrmeisters. Banner then transported Coffers and the newborn from the bridge to the Beatrice Hospital.'"

Newt watched me over the top of the magazine. "That's an accurate statement and I'd like to remind you that I'm not on trial here."

"Not yet," I said, dropping the file in a chair.

He put the magazine down. "What's that supposed to mean?"

"Newt," I said, my voice ragged, "you talked to the doctor at the hospital. You knew she was in no shape to leave the baby at the bridge."

"Did she ever say 'I didn't leave the baby at the bridge.' Did she? Did she ever tell you that? Answer that." Newt's voice was rising.

"No, you answer this!" I put both hands on the desk and leaned toward him. "If Karl Kittman hadn't come over the hill when he did, and if he hadn't seen Mitch holding the baby, would Mitch have left the baby there to die or would he have left Jessica *and* the baby to die?"

Newt stood up, his eyes glaring. "If Mitch Banner hadn't had the decency to take that girl in, and if she hadn't done what she did, he never would have found himself in that predicament."

White hot rage flooded through me and my arm cleared the desk of the magazines as well as a stapler and an in-basket. Newt's hand went to his holster. "You told me Jessica had motive," I said leaning further over the empty desk, "but who would have wanted Trent Green dead? Would that be *your* primary suspect, Jessica Coffers, who would have been cleared of everything she's been accused of? Or Mitch Banner, who would have faced charges of attempted murder and statutory rape?"

"Do not raise your voice to me," he warned.

Newt kept talking but I picked up my file and walked toward the door. I went back up both flights of stairs to my office.

I put the file back in the cabinet and looked at the clock. They should be here any minute. I heard the door to the second floor open and I went to my office door. Newt stood in the public waiting area outside my door, his blue eyes filled with rage. "Don't walk away from me when I'm talking to you," he said "and don't ever touch anything on my desk again."

Dot stood behind the counter, both she and the people she'd been waiting on were watching us.

I went back in my office. Newt followed and shut the door.

"Mitch Banner is not a murderer. He's a good man who made a mistake," Newt said.

"Tell it to the judge. Literally," I said.

"No, let me tell you something. I did talk to that doctor, and then I went and talked to Jessica. That girl's concern wasn't who got charged, her concern was that she continue to stay at the Banner's. She's the one who's screwed up."

Anger surged through me and I took a step closer to Newt. "So, as the judge and the jury of a fifteen-year-old girl, you covered everything up," I said.

"I didn't cover anything up! My report is accurate. If it's not the whole story, it's because there was no cooperation from the witnesses," he said.

"Wendell had the whole story," I said. "He told me it's in his file in the storage room. Newt, don't you get it? That's the file Trent wanted me to see! Do you have keys to Trent's office? We could go down there right now and see if that file is still there. If it's gone, it's because Mitch Banner took it when he killed Trent Green!"

Newt's voice was level and certain. "I know Mitch Banner and he is not a killer. He did not kill Trent Green." He looked toward the door and then back at me. "Have you ever heard the saying, 'the road to hell is paved with good intentions?' Well, that was the road Mitch took. He had nothing but good intentions it took him to hell."

My phone rang and we both jumped. We looked at each other and thought the same thing: *Jessica.*

"Out," I said. I went back to my desk to answer the phone.

Newt turned back to me when he reached the door. "She pled to child endangerment. She never accused Mitch of anything," he said. "Don't put words in her mouth now that weren't there before."

"State Probation Office," I said into the phone.

"Gillian Jones, please," a male voice said.

"This is Gillian," I sat down at the desk.

Newt was still standing there with his hand on the doorknob. I pointed and mouthed, "out." He left, leaving the door open behind him.

"This is Investigator Cottel from the Omaha Police Department," he said. "You filed a supplemental missing persons report on Lark McCallister?"

"Yes," I said.

"This is a courtesy call to let you know we've got a body. We're waiting for confirmation on the identity," he said. "Sorry," he added.

"Do you need someone to identity the body?" I asked.

"Umm, no, we wouldn't do that," he said.

"Where was she found?" I asked.

"Down by the Missouri River. Her car was in a parking lot at a restaurant by the river. Someone noticed it hadn't been moved in a couple of days and called it in," he said. "When the plates came back to McCallister, we sent a couple officers down there and they did a search. She was in the ditch between the service road and the river. Someone had weighted down a trash bag on the end of the body so you couldn't really see it."

My head suddenly throbbed. "Do you know the cause of death," I asked.

"The medical examiner on the scene said it appears that a lot of her bones were broken. She might have fallen a good distance or," he paused, "more than likely she was hit by a car and knocked to the place where she was found. It doesn't look like the body's been moved."

"You're treating it as a homicide?" I said.

"Oh, definitely," he replied. "And I have a question for you. In the initial report, the one called in first, one of her co-workers said the victim was meeting someone to 'light some fireworks that should have gone off a long time ago.' Do you know what she meant, or who she was going to meet?"

"I don't know who she was meeting," I said. "But she had a cell phone and I have her number," I said. "If she was meeting someone, there might be a . . ."

"We're on that," he said. "Her cell phone wasn't on her, but her roommate is in the process of printing her call log off the Internet and is bringing it in. It's faster than going through the phone company."

Her roommate. "The roommate, LaShawn," I said, "she knows you've found the body?"

"Yes, she knows," he paused. "Hopefully, we'll have someone arrested soon," he said.

"Hopefully," I repeated, and then told him it might be related to an attack on me the previous Tuesday. I gave him Sid's number to get the details.

"Let me give you my number in case something else occurs to you," he said. I scribbled his number on my desk calendar and said goodbye. I felt the back of my eyes throb. I put my head down on my desk.

"Ma'am?" There was concern in the soft southern lilt. I looked up to see Jessica standing in the doorway. "Are you okay?" she asked.

"Jessica," I said. "Come in and shut the door.

TWENTY-FIVE

"Where's Logan?" I asked.

"He's having an ice cream with Kay down at Gap's," she said.

"Why did you leave him with Kay? I asked you to bring Logan with you," I said.

"Kay thought it'd be easier if I did the drug test without having to watch him." She paused. "Is everything alright, ma'am?"

"Yes," I said. Maybe it was better Logan wasn't here right now. My mind felt foggy. I picked up my pen. "Jessica," I said. "I'm not going to do a drug test, but there are some questions that have come up. I need you to answer them truthfully."

"I didn't kill Trent Green," she said.

"I don't believe you did," I said. "But I do want you to tell me what happened when Logan was born."

She shook her head ever so slightly.

"Are you afraid of someone?" I asked gently.

"No, ma'am," she said.

"Are you afraid of Mitch?" I asked.

She shook her head.

"Then tell me what happened the day Logan was born," I said again.

Her slight shake of the head was reminiscent of Logan.

"Jessica," I said, sitting back in my chair, "I'm going to order a paternity test for Mitch. Then you won't have to say anything, we'll just let the evidence speak for itself."

"No! Please, don't." My heart ached at the anguish in her voice.

"Jessica, I can't let you live with someone who raped you." I physically cringed at the thought it might still be happening.

"No. Please! It wasn't like that," she said.

"Then tell me what happened," I said.

I posed my pen to write and I could hear Jessica shifting in her chair. "Remember the ice storm last December?" she asked.

"Yes," I said, thinking back to last December.

"Kay had gone to Denver because their daughter was moving. Kay's flight got cancelled because of the weather," Jessica's voice had kept the accent and lost the lilt.

"Okay," I said.

"We lost our electricity, and then, I don't know, it just happened," she said.

"It just happened once?" I asked.

"No, a couple of times."

I was chilled by her matter of fact tone. "It ended when Kay came back home?"

"No," she shook her head "It ended before that. It ended when he asked me if I loved him."

"What did you say?"

"I said, 'no, sir,'"

"And he said?"

"Nothing at first. Then he said he was sorry and it was all his fault. He said it would never happen again and he asked me to forgive him," she said.

"You remember him saying all that?" I asked, looking across the desk at her.

The serious Jessica had returned. "He's the only grownup who every apologized to me," she said.

I took a breath. "And it didn't happen again?"

"No, ma'am, it didn't."

"And you broke up with your boyfriend when you realized you were pregnant?"

"Yes, ma'am," she said.

"And Brandon knows he's not the father so there's no reason for him to respond to any questions or paperwork about his parental rights," I said.

"Yes, ma'am."

"Did you tell anyone you were pregnant?"

Jessica paused. "No, ma'am. No one around here, ma'am."

"But you told someone. Who did you tell?" I asked.

"Santana," she said.

"Who's Santana?" I asked.

"We used to live together at a group home," Jessica said.

"That's the friend you said was like a sister?" I asked.

She nodded. "There were a lot of mean people at that home and we used to watch out for each other."

"Why did you tell Santana and no one else?"

"Because she had an apartment and Logan and I were going to go live with her. She's a year older than me," she added.

"But that didn't happen?" I asked.

"They said she stole something at a store and she went to jail instead," Jessica said. "I still was going to go stay with her. I just thought I had more time before the baby came."

"What happened that night at the bridge?" I asked.

She paused. "I don't remember much about the bridge," she said.

"Tell me what you do remember," I said.

She didn't say anything for a little bit. "I thought I was going to die," she said. "I remember Mitch coming into the bathroom and there was a lot of blood. He picked Logan up and said we had to get everything cleaned up before Kay got home."

"So he cleaned it up?" I said.

"No, then he said we needed to get to a doctor. Then I was lying in the back of the car and that's all I remember until we're at the hospital."

"Jessica, why didn't you tell someone this before?"

The slight tilt of the chin. "I want to stay with the Banners," she said.

"But with all you go through at school? And even after . . ."

"It's the best home I've ever had," she said. "And I have to have someplace safe to stay on account of Logan. I want to raise Logan myself. Kay and Mitch let me do that."

I closed my eyes. I'd been so wrong. All along I thought Jessica and I had so much in common and now I realized I'd been looking for a family that loved me and Jessica had been looking for a refuge.

"Ma'am, are you sure you're okay?"

I opened my eyes and tried to smile. "I'm just not feeling very good right now. I'd like you to go get Logan and bring him here so I can see him and make sure he's okay, and then our probation visit is over."

"Should I just call Kay? She's got a cell phone," Jessica said.

"No, I don't think I should see Kay right now," I said. "Just go get Logan."

"Yes, ma'am," she said.

I watched Jessica walk out of the office and waited to hear the glass door open. I flipped open my rolodex and dialed Mary Lee's office phone. Her voice came onto the line, "I'm either away from my desk or. . ." I slammed the receiver down. I punched in her cell phone number.

She answered on the first ring.

"This is Gillian Jones. I want Jessica Coffers in protective custody."

"What? It's Friday afternoon. Can't we talk about this on Monday? I know Jessica's been on the hot seat lately, but I'm on my way to Falls City right now."

"Mary Lee, listen to me. Mitch Banner is Logan's father. I want her placed in protective custody! Now!"

"Mitch?" Mary Lee said and then nothing.

"Mary Lee? Are you there?"

"Hold on, I'm turning around in the middle of the highway," she said. I waited until she came back on the line. "Gillian, are you sure about this, because if you're not . . ."

"She just admitted to me that Mitch was Logan's father."

There was a pause. "Where is she?" Mary Lee asked.

"She and Logan will be in my office any minute," I said.

"Keep them there. I'm on my way." She hung up.

I put the phone back in its cradle.

Minutes later, Jessica came back in the office with Logan on her hip. "Here he is," she said.

"Would you shut the door, please?" I asked. I rolled my chair toward the little refrigerator.

"He just had ice cream, ma'am," she said. "He shouldn't have a juice. It's too much sugar."

"Right," I said. I took some wooden blocks out of my bottom drawer and came around the desk. I put the blocks on the floor for Logan to play with and pulled up a chair by the one Jessica had been sitting in. "Please sit down," I said.

She paused, and then sat down.

"First of all, I'm sorry," I said.

"You're taking Logan?" she said, panic in her voice.

"No, I'd never do that. I'll do whatever it takes to keep you and Logan together, but not with the Banners."

"But ma'am, we don't want to leave," she said.

"I know. I understand that." Logan wriggled around to look at me. "Jessica, I want you to ask yourself who would want Trent Green dead?"

"I don't know," she said, the worry line creasing her forehead.

"I think Trent Green knew Mitch was Logan's father, too. If Mitch knew that, don't you think he'd want to keep Trent quiet? If the truth came out, Mitch would be the one facing charges. He probably wouldn't want Kay to know the truth, either."

She blinked back tears. "He didn't kill Trent Green, and Kay already knows about Logan."

"She does?" I asked. "She knows Mitch is Logan's father?"

Jessica nodded. "She knows. Mitch told her what had happened after she came back from Denver. She cried at first. Then she was mad and said she was going to kick us both out. Mitch said he was sorry and then she said she wasn't going to throw away thirty years of a good marriage. After that, she said she was going to send me away but Mitch said it wasn't fair to me, that it was his fault. They talked about it and they said I could live there until I finished high school. After that I'd need to move." Logan stopped playing with the blocks and crawled into her lap.

I was speechless. "They both know," I repeated weakly.

"Yes, ma'am," she said, a tear running down her cheek. Logan watched the tear and followed it with his finger.

"Neither of them knew you were pregnant, though?"

"No, ma'am. I was going to leave before the baby came, but then Santana went to jail and Logan came sooner than I thought."

"Why were you going to leave before the baby came?" I asked.

"Because I didn't think they'd want the baby, and I didn't know where he'd get sent," Jessica sniffed.

"And after Logan was born?" I asked.

"They said we could both stay. It's a good home, ma'am. We like it there." Logan pointed towards the blocks and she put him back on the floor.

A lump had formed in my throat and I had to swallow before I could talk. "Jessica, someone saw the Banner's black Taurus driving away from Trent's house after he was killed," I said. "I think it was Mitch driving away."

She shook her head. "No. Newt already asked about that. Mitch was at the sale barn in Beatrice." Logan pushed back down off her lap and went back to the blocks.

"Did Newt ask where you were?"

"Yes, ma'am. I told him I had been at Mr. Green's office earlier in the day but I went straight home afterward."

So Newt had considered Mitch as a suspect, I wondered if Newt had checked out Mitch's alibi. "Jessica, I want you to think about what Mitch had at stake here. Wasn't Mitch the person who wanted you to put Logan up for adoption? Don't you think he wanted you to do that to protect himself?"

She shook her head. "Foster care," she said. "Mitch said you and your husband would be the foster parents and Logan would be in foster care. He said I could still see Logan and then when I aged out of foster care, I'd be able to take Logan back and raise him myself."

My office phone rang.

Logan looked up from the blocks and said "lo."

I reached across the desk. "State Probation Office," I said.

"Gillian," Clint said. "What are you doing at your office? It's after five and we're supposed to be at the hall at 6:30."

"Something's come up," I said. "I'll meet you there."

"What do you mean something's come up?" he asked.

"Just grab the Danish and I'll meet you there at 6:30," I said and hung up the phone.

"Can we go home?" Jessica asked, quiet desperation in her voice.

I winced at the plea in her voice. "No," I said. "We're going to wait for Mary Lee to get here and then you'll be in protective custody."

"With Logan?" she asked.

"With Logan," I said.

"Isn't protective custody a temporary place?" she asked. "What about after protective custody?"

"You and Logan are going to be together in a safe place," I said. "I promise."

"But we're safe at the Banner's house," she said.

"You'll both be safe," I said. "And together. I promise you that."

TWENTY-SIX

I parked my car at our house and walked to the hall since it was a block away. I took a proffered program and looked around for Clint. Russ Johanson was coming in the hall to join his family and he gave me a friendly wave.

It was five minutes before the musical was to start. The folding chairs were mostly full and people around me were standing in clusters looking for places to sit.

"Come on," Clint said, stepping up beside me and taking my hand, "Mom's saved us seats up front." He pulled me forward, "What happened that you couldn't leave the courthouse earlier?"

The stage is at one end of the auditorium and the kitchen is off to the side. Tables in front of the kitchen area were loaded with desserts and several large silver coffee urns lined the kitchen counters. "There's too much to tell, but I think I know who killed Trent Green," I said.

"Clint!" a man shouted and I swung around. He gave me a questioning look, and then said, "Clint, would you help us set up some more chair? We're running out of places for people to sit."

"Save me a place," Clint said as I continued toward the front.

I noticed Trudy March was already seated, talking animatedly to the woman sitting in back of her. I resisted the urge to go over and tell her how wrong she'd been about Jessica. I saw my sister-in-law Linda and her husband sitting front and center, next to an anxious-looking Marlene.

"Oh, Gillian, there you are!" Marlene said. Her hair was freshly done and her dress glittered under the lights. She looked around. "Now we've lost Clint," she said worriedly.

"He's coming," I assured her. "He's helping to set up more chairs. You look great," I added, sitting down beside Frank.

"Hello, Gillian," Georgia Lohrmeister was in the seat behind me. She put her hand on my shoulder.

I turned around. "Hello, Georgia."

"Poor Linda, she's just a wreck," Georgia said.

I looked over at my sister-in-law who was twisting a Kleenex in her hands. "What's the matter with Linda?" I asked.

"Ashley has butterflies like you wouldn't believe! This morning she thought she was going to be ill and didn't know if she'd be able to perform tonight," Georgia leaned forward to speak to me in a whisper. "I told her not to worry. My daughter, Brenda, was the lead in the first musical they had, and she was positively sick to her stomach. There was so much pressure! Everyone wondered if she was going to be able to pull it off. Well, let me tell you, once she got out there, she did just fine and it will be the same for Ashley." She nodded and sat back in her chair.

I felt a little sick to my stomach, too. "I think I know how she felt," I said, turning back to face the stage.

The door by the stage opened and a young man in a pleated headdress and a pleated toga stepped out. "Mom," he said as a woman hurried up and handed him a pair of brown flip flops. "Thanks," he said to her. And then to me, "Hello, Mrs. Jones."

"Hello, Anthony," I responded, recognizing him as a former probation client who'd been ticketed for MIP, trespassing and several other charges that went along with starting a bonfire on someone else's property, and then inviting other minors over for beer. "I'm glad to see you're in the musical." I smiled.

"Yep," he smiled back. "I've got one of the fun parts. I'm Pharaoh."

The door to the stage opened again and a blond girl, her blue eyes outlined in charcoal, stepped out in a toga sans pleats. She held the door open and sang in perfect pitch, *"Phar-aoh. Oh, Pahr-aoh, you are wanted backstage."*

She then gave Marlene and the people seated in the front row a haughty glance. Madison O'Malley, I thought to myself.

"See you Mrs. Jones," Anthony said, raising a hand.

"Break a leg," I responded.

They both went inside the stage door. I looked behind me. The group of people waiting to be seated had disappeared and so had Clint. The auditorium lights dimmed along with the murmur of the audience. Clint slid into the seat beside me. "They're running behind, it should have started five minutes ago," he whispered.

With that, Pastor Jim stepped in front of the heavy red velvet curtains. "Thank you all for coming tonight and, without further ado, I'd like to present this year's musical, *Annie Get Your Commandments*!"

The auditorium filled with polite applause and Pastor Jim disappeared behind the curtain. A minute later the curtains opened to piano music and a chorus line marched from both sides of the stage.

"There's no commandments, like the ten commandments!
"They're the best commandments we know!"

As the chorus lines merged into one, a smiling Ashley stepped forward in the middle of the stage and sang in a clear, strong voice:

"Everything about them is redeeming!
"All you'll need is some believing!"

I looked past Frank and saw Linda's hands relax on the Kleenex as Marlene patted her on the arm. I turned my attention back to Ashley.

"Pharaoh said we would not go far,
"In the desert, without a car,
"But the Red Sea parted, and here we are!"

Clint leaned over and whispered in my ear, "I don't think Ashley's smile is genuine, but at least it's there."

I nodded. My stomach was still in knots and I was feeling more nauseous by the minute. I leaned back and closed my eyes.

"Are you okay?" Clint whispered.

"I'm not feeling the best," I whispered. "I'll tell you about it after the musical." I leaned back in my chair and listened as Ashley sang her solo number, "I Am A Philistine, Too." The rest of the musical went by in a haze and it only seemed a short time later that Clint was nudging me in the ribs, urging me to stand up and applaud with everyone else. The house lights came up and Marlene hurried to the stage door. The cast assembled across the stage for another round of applause while Pastor Jim stepped toward center stage with a microphone.

"And let's not forget the students who helped with props and scenery!" He held his hand out as several other young people came onstage and the applause became louder. Marlene joined the group, a plaque in her hands. The sequins on her dress glittered in the lights.

"Now," Pastor Jim said into the microphone, "when we are done applauding these individuals, we have someone else that deserves our attention." The applause died down and Pastor Jim signaled everyone to sit down. "I should start by mentioning that this is the twenty-fifth year in Bend Brook for our summer musical. Now, I know some of you are thinking, 'Pastor Jim cannot be that old,'" he stopped to chuckle and a few people in the audience tittered, "but you are wrong. Twenty-seven ago, I met a man who assisted with youth ministry at a congregation in Nebraska City."

I took Clint's arm and he put his hand on mine.

Pastor Jim continued. "Well, there I was wondering what the heck I could do to get our young people excited about church, so I asked for suggestions. Lo and behold, this generous individual suggested a play or a musical. Doubting Thomas that I was, I told him I didn't think I could do it. Then when I came to Bend Brook a couple of years later, I found myself wondering again how was I going to get the youth involved in our church. So I picked up the phone and called Scott and the rest is history. For the last twenty-five years Scott Torrance has shown up faithfully ever summer."

Someone in the audience applauded prematurely. "No, no, wait, I'm not done," Pastor Jim said, and the audience laughed. "Scott," he continued, "has assisted me with each and every musical that we've done in Bend Brook. No, I take that back. He does more than assist, he runs the show."

My mouth had gone dry and my legs felt like rubber.

"Scott, get up here and take a bow," Pastor said to the unseen person behind the piano. "And, folks," he turned back to the audience, "just to give you an example of what a trouper he is, he has been sitting over there playing the piano with a banged-up hand. Now, Scott plays the piano like a professional and his lovely wife convinced him that was his calling, but he's a mechanic at heart and is always doing something or the other to his car. Well, to make a long story short, he was working on his car this week and the darn thing wasn't in gear. The car got away from him, but not before banging up his hand. I think if it would have been just between him and the car, the car would have won, but a tree got involved, and if you see the front of his car, it looks to me like the tree got the best of them both." He stopped to chuckle and then looked back at the piano. "Scott, stop hiding your light under a basket and get up here to accept this award!"

I felt something run down the side of my face. I put my hand up to feel sweat.

The person behind the piano slowly stood. He walked toward Marlene and Pastor Jim. His right hand was bandaged.

"Scott Torrance, everyone!" Pastor Jim said. Everyone stood and applauded.

Marlene took the microphone from Pastor Jim. "And now, on behalf of the congregation, we'd like you to accept this plaque in appreciation of your dedication and commitment." She handed him the plaque.

Scott looked around the audience and then he glanced at me. When my eyes met his, I knew it was the same person who'd been at the storage unit. I sat down and pulled my purse onto my lap. My cell phone was in my purse. I needed to call Sid.

"Gillian," Clint sat back down by me, "what's the matter?"

"I need . . ." my purse slipped to the floor. "I think I'm going to faint," I said, putting my head between my knees.

TWENTY-SEVEN

"Drink this," Harvey, a co-worker of Clint's who was also an EMT, offered me a Styrofoam cup of water. I was still sitting in the folding chair, with Clint at my side and Marlene hovering over me.

I took a sip of the water.

"Do you think you need to go the emergency room?" he asked.

"No, I'm okay," I said. "Just a little woozy."

"Do you think she's pregnant?" Marlene asked Harvey.

Harvey's eyebrows went up. "I have no way of knowing that, but I am fairly certain she is dehydrated."

"She missed supper," Clint said. "And she said she wasn't feeling well earlier."

"She's pregnant!" Marlene said happily.

"Or dehydrated," Harvey said, gently taking my wrist and poking his finger on the underside of my arm.

"But most likely pregnant," Marlene said.

"Look at the indentation my finger is leaving in her flesh," Harvey said. That's a sign she hasn't gotten enough fluid. I'm pretty sure she's dehydrated."

"Pregnant!" Marlene snapped.

"Mom," Clint pointed across the auditorium, "it looks like Georgia needs help at the dessert table."

"Oh, dear," Marlene said, "I am supposed to be helping with the desserts." She looked at me, then back at the tables, indecision on her face.

"Mom, go on over and help Georgia," Clint said. "Gillian will be all right."

"I'm sure Georgia could use you right now," I added.

Clint turned to me after his mother had left. "How much did you have to drink today?"

"I had some iced tea, maybe half a glass or so," I said.

"And?" Clint asked.

"That's it."

"Dehydrated," Harvey said with authority.

"Actually, I think she was trying to tell me she needed a glass of water right before she sat down," Clint said to Harvey.

Suddenly, I remembered what I needed to do. "No, I was trying to tell you I need to make a phone call." I drank the rest of the water and put the empty cup on a chair. Clint held out his hand. I took it and stood up. I looked around the auditorium. There were clusters of people gathered around the dessert tables, others sat in folding chairs balancing plates and cups in their laps.

"Where's Scott Torrance?" I asked.

"I don't know," Clint looked around. "Pastor Jim's over there with Ashley and the rest of the cast. Scott just sort of disappeared." Clint walked over to the edge of the stage. "Look, his plaque is still here. He must be around here somewhere." Clint came back over to me. "Why do you need to see him?"

"I'll explain on the way home," I said.

"That's a good idea," Harvey said. He picked up the first aide kit. "Home is where you should be right now. Drinking lots of water," he added.

Clint and I started walking toward the doors. "Do you need a ride?" Marlene called from the dessert table.

"No, Mom, it's only a block," Clint said.

My eyes searched the groups of people in the auditorium, but there was no sign of Scott. The hot, humid air enveloped us once we stepped outside. "We've got to be careful," I said. "It was Scott Torrance who attacked me at the storage unit. I know he killed Lark McCallister, too."

"Uh, Gillian, I'm pretty sure you do have heat stroke because before the musical you said you knew who killed Trent Green," Clint ended with a nervous laugh.

"I know who killed Trent, too," I said. "We've got to get home." We started walking faster.

"Are you sure you're okay?" Clint asked. "Why do you think Scott would kill Lark or attack you?"

"Because Lark knew Scott Torrance was the one who tried to rape JoJo. And Scott probably raped other girls from Bend Brook."

"Are you sure?"

I tightened my grip on Clint's arm. "When I was at the storage unit, I pushed the door shut on the guy's fingers."

"Oh, that's right," Clint said. "Scott's fingers were taped. And, you know, it was really strange how he just sat there even after Pastor Jim said his name. Was that when you knew?"

"He looked right at me after he stood up. He knows I know. That's why we've got to be careful."

We were within yards of our house when Coco bounded forward and gave a welcoming bark. Clint and I both stopped. I involuntarily shuddered despite the heat.

"Let's get inside and I'll turn the outside lights on," Clint said. We went up the porch steps and into the kitchen. Clint walked through the house to make sure everything was secure while I got a glass of water. "Everything looks okay," Clint said. "I'm going to check outside while you call Bob."

Bob. I'd forgotten about Bob. I spilled some of the water.

"Are you feeling faint again?" Clint rushed over to me.

"No. I forgot about Bob," I said.

"But . . ."

"It's Sid that I need to call," I said. "He needs to know Scott killed Lark."

"But then don't you need to let Bob know, too?" Clint asked. "Especially if they arrest Scott for Lark's murder, don't you think he should hear it from you and not on the news?"

I took a drink of water. "You're right," I said. "I'll call Sid first, and then Bob."

The call to Sid was quick. Once I told him about Scott's bandaged hand and Nebraska City, Sid all but hung up on me. I found Bob's number in the phone book and wondered if it was too late to call. It was nearly ten o'clock. I punched the numbers and he picked up after the third ring.

I gave him the condensed version of Scott being the person who attempted to rape JoJo. I started with Lark's statement that JoJo had said it was someone from church and ended with Scott's abrupt departure after tonight's musical.

Bob said nothing when I was finished.

"Scott Torrance," I said. "He's the man who assists Pastor Jim with the summer musicals."

"I know who he is," Bob answered. "But if JoJo knew, why didn't she tell me or Russ? Why didn't that no-good roommate say something?"

"JoJo probably wanted to protect you," I said. I decided this wasn't the moment to tell Bob the no-good roommate was dead.

Silence.

"Bob, are you there?" I asked.

"What's going to happen to him now?" he asked.

"As far as JoJo, probably nothing. But I've already called a police officer so they're aware of it," I said.

"I still don't understand. . ." Bob trailed off. "There was that call on Christmas Day from the man who asked for JoJo. She was so happy and then the next day . . ."

I sighed. "I can explain the call, but it may not be what you want to hear." I spent the next few minutes breaking the news about Jonathan and the lunch date that hadn't been a date at all, but a meeting to tell JoJo she had been exposed to AIDS. I waited for Bob to say something when I finished.

"It was what I needed to know so I can go on," he said.

"There's one more thing," I said. Lark had a storage unit and JoJo's artwork and mementos are there, as well as some furniture. I don't know what will happen now that . . ."

"Rob and Russ can go through it," Bob interrupted me and I was relieved to hear a stronger, take-charge tone in his voice.

"Well, I'll let you handle that," I said.

"Thank you for looking into this for me," he said and hung up the phone.

TWENTY-EIGHT

It was Clint's Saturday to work. He had offered to stay home with me, but I didn't think it was necessary. The night had been uneventful and I was feeling better this morning. I was sitting on the back porch, sipping water, and waiting for some news. Coco loped over to me with her Frisbee and gave a minor struggle when I took it away to throw it across the yard.

My cell phone was in my pocket and I took it out just to make sure I hadn't missed a call. I was worried about Jessica and Logan. I looked at my cell phone again. Shouldn't Mary Lee call to let me know where they were and how they were doing?

Coco returned with the Frisbee and I threw it just as my cell phone rang. I checked the number, it was Sid.

"Hello," I said.

"Gillian, where exactly are you?" he asked.

"I'm home," I answered.

"Good. Listen, I've got an update for you. Last night, after you called with that info on Scott Torrance, I called OPD to leave a message for the investigator on Lark's case. Well, I got some kid who is assisting with the case. He started running personal information on Scott."

"And he found something?" my heartbeat quickened.

"He found Scott has a '96 Impala SS registered to him. Well, coincidentally, the Nebraska State Patrol is looking for that make of car. And why, you might you ask, would the State Patrol be looking for such a car?"

"Because of evidence they found on Lark's body?"

"That'll probably be true, too, but no, the reason they were looking for that type of car is because they believe it's connected to the Trent Green homicide."

"Wait," I said. "Trent's murder? I'm not following this," I said.

"Let me go back," Sid said. "When the killer dumped Green's briefcase in the ditch, he turned around on the gravel road to go back to the highway. One of the troopers saw a tire print in the soft dirt on the shoulder of the road and made a cast of the tire track. They had an eyewitness who said the Banner's black Taurus was seen leaving the scene of the crime, but the tire didn't fit with the Taurus. It's a wider tire that will only fit certain vehicles and the Impala is one of them."

"What color is Scott's car?" I asked.

"You tell me," Sid said.

"Black?"

"Bingo," Sid answered.

"Scott thought Trent Green had gotten a hold of police reports about the rape victims in Bend Brook, so he killed him," I said.

"Another bingo," Sid said.

"But the night Lark was killed, wasn't Scott with his wife at a music program in Lincoln? You said his picture was in the paper."

"So it was. The photographer should of stuck around because they went in and they came right back out. People who were at the program said the wife wasn't feeling good. He took her home and put her to bed. If she went to sleep right away, it would have given him a free night, so to speak."

"Sid, the police reports that Trent wanted me to look at?"

"Yeah, nothings been found yet," Sid said. "But as I hear it, they did find some other paperwork blowing around in that field so it might still turn up."

"I don't think there's anything there. I think the report Trent wanted me to see was a file on one of my probation clients."

Sid was silent for a moment. "When did this change? I thought Trent Green had found reports on the assaults."

"I did, too. Until yesterday."

"Well, it's water under the bridge now," Sid said. "Scott Torrance has murdered two people."

"They have enough to arrest him?" I asked.

"If they can find him. They got a judge out of bed early this morning to sign a search warrant for Torrance's house and vehicles. About three hours ago, they swooped."

"They've got him?" I asked.

"No. Scott Torrance was gone, as was his car. Torrance's wife said he left before six this morning. She said someone called for him last night and he needed to go to Bend Brook to finish up things with the musical."

"Is he with Pastor Jim?" I asked.

"Nope," Sid replied. "The Pastor said he had no plans to see Scott today."

"Did he lie about the phone call so he could leave?" I asked.

"No, the wife heard the phone ring, too, at about a quarter to eleven last night. She said he was on the phone for a while, maybe ten minutes. The caller ID's been deleted, though."

"Did they find anything else?"

"It's what they didn't find. While the house was being searched, the wife discovered the cash they keep on hand is gone. The wife checked their joint account and the small amount of money he had access to is gone."

"I thought you said the family had money," I said.

"They do. He doesn't."

"And she has no idea where he went?" I asked.

"She swears up and down she doesn't," Sid said.

"Can you track him by his cell phone?" I asked.

"His cell phone was in the fish pond by their front door," Sid replied. "He's a tricky little bastard. And that's one of the things I'm calling to tell you: he's got nothing to lose so he's making a run for it. It's like having a loose cannon out there."

"Do you think he's in Bend Brook?" I asked.

"No. I don't. I just want you to know he's out there somewhere and to be careful."

You'll call me when he's caught?" I asked.

"I'm figuring out how to put your number on speed dial as we speak," Sid said.

I disconnected and felt a queasy feeling in my stomach. It wasn't from lack of water, it was the sick feeling you get when you make a mistake and I had made a big one. Newt had been right and I had been wrong. Mitch Banner wasn't a killer, at least he hadn't killed Trent Green. What he intended to do at the bridge that night was another matter, but that had been two years ago and Jessica still felt safe at the Banners. Wasn't that the word she had used, safe? Was she safe now? Was Logan? I started scrolling through the numbers in my cell phone to see if Mary Lee's cell phone number was there.

An older style pickup slowed down as it reached our driveway and then backed up to the mailbox. I walked around the side of the house as Bob Johanson was pulling the mailbox open.

"Bob!" I yelled and waved my arm.

Bob somberly held up an envelope in acknowledgement.

I opened the gate and grabbed Coco's collar as she tried to squeeze past me.

"I've got a letter for you," Bob said with grim determination.

"Would you like to come in?" I asked, holding Coco back from jumping on the pickup.

"No," Bob shook his head. "I'm due at the church in fifteen minutes."

I stood there awkwardly. "I hope you aren't upset. I didn't know if I should tell you about JoJo or not," I said.

"I needed to know," he said.

The awkward silence was back. "She had a lot of artistic talent," I said. "Her paintings were beautiful."

"I wanted you to find out the things I didn't know," he said, "not the things I did." He took a breath and I watched his shirt deflate as he exhaled. "I've got one more thing I'd like you to do. It's written down here." He handed me the envelope.

"You can just tell me," I said.

"No," he said, staring straight ahead. "I'm due at the church. Read it after I'm gone and make sure you follow the directions."

I watched as the pickup pulled away. I dragged Coco back into the yard and went into the house. I slit the letter open and pulled out a folded sheet of paper. A check fluttered out and landed on the dining room table. I looked at the amount: Three hundred dollars. Hadn't I told Bob I wasn't a private investigator and it would be illegal for me to accept money? What was he doing?

I picked up the sheet of paper and saw the spidery handwriting. *This money is to make sure he's charged with murder.* That didn't make sense. I looked at the check, it was written on the Johanson Farm Account. Rob would know his dad had written me a check, too.

I got my purse and keys. I'd go to the church and give Bob his check back.

TWENTY-NINE

The church was a picturesque white building just off the highway south of town. It has the traditional stained glass windows, the steeple with a bell, and a shady cemetery directly behind it. A stand of trees on the side of the parking lot obscured my vision of the entire parking lot, but as I approached, I saw that there were two cars at the end of the lot. One was Bob's pickup and the other one was a black car. My heart thudded in my chest. I pulled my cell phone out of my purse and punched "send" to dial the last call that had been received.

"Yeah?" Sid asked.

"There's a black car at the church, I think it might be Scott's," I said with urgency. "The church is about two miles south of Bend Brook, on the highway to Kansas,"

"Got the location," Sid said. "Is it an Impala?" he asked.

"I'm not close enough to see. Bob Johanson's pickup is here, too." I turned onto the gravel road and approached the parking lot. I could see Bob standing in the parking lot, a brown bag in his hand. Scott Torrance stood a foot or two away from Bob, a gun in his hand. "He's got a gun!" I yelled and threw the cell phone on the passenger seat.

I grabbed the steering wheel with both hands, veered into the parking lot, stomped on the accelerator and aimed for Scott. He turned the gun toward me. Bob stepped toward him and grabbed Scott's arm. I slammed on the brakes, not wanting to hit Bob, and skidded sideways to a halt. A bullet hit the passenger side of my windshield and it shattered. Scott threw Bob to the ground and ran toward the church.

I got out, went over to Bob and pulled him behind my car. "Are you all right?" I asked.

"You," Bob was having trouble breathing, "leave. Now."

I propped Bob against the tire. "He'll kill you!" I said.

Bob nodded. His breathing was easier but still short and labored. "I called him. Told him I had cancer and wanted to give him $4,000 for everything he's done for the church."

I realized the bag was full of money.

"Rob and I do grinding on a cash basis," he wheezed. "Used to, just Rob now."

"Bob, you brought him money? Why would you . . ."

Bob's voice was weak yet stern. "I brought my money. I just didn't tell him he was going to have to kill me to get it. And then you," he stopped for breath.

"Me?" I said.

"Didn't follow directions. You were supposed to make sure he was charged with murder." He took a breath. "After he killed me."

"He *is* going to be charged with murder. He'll be charged for killing Trent Green *and* Lark."

"Lark's dead?" Bob asked.

"Lark made plans to meet him and he killed her," I said, glancing around the side of the car to see where Scott had gone.

"Why would," he took a breath, "Lark meet him?"

"Probably for the same reason you're meeting him! She probably wanted to make sure he was properly punished."

Bob leaned back and closed his eyes. A grimace spread across his face.

"Are you in pain?" I asked.

He shook his head, and I realized it was a smile, not a grimace. "JoJo was right all along," he said. "She always said Lark and I," he paused to breathe, "had more in common that we'd ever know." He guffawed.

My car was in the middle of the parking lot and Bob and I were between it and the stand of trees. The pickup and the black Impala were at the end of the parking lot, closer to the road. "His car is the closest one to the road," I said. "If we shift around to the front of the car, he could leave."

Bob pointed weakly to the bag of money in response.

I took the money and heaved the bag over my car. "Take the money and go," I yelled. After a few heartbeats I heard footsteps crunch on gravel. The footsteps on the gravel was reminiscent of the sound at the storage unit and it sent chills down my spine. I peeked over the driver's door to see where Scott was and a bullet pinged off my car.

"He's got the bag of money," I said. "He'll leave now."

Bob closed his eyes and nodded.

We waited. I heard footsteps on the gravel. "He's coming closer," I whispered to Bob.

"I have a spare gun. In the truck," Bob said, his eyes still closed. "Under the driver's seat."

"A spare gun?" I asked. "You bought a spare? Are you saying you gave Scott the gun he has?"

Bob nodded. "He had to shoot me to get the money."

The footsteps retreated toward the church. Why didn't he just go to his car, he had the money. "What kind of gun?" I asked.

"Pistol. Loaded. Easy to shoot," Bob paused for a breath, "line up the sights."

The pickup was closest to my car. I peeked over the top of the car and ran over to the pickup. I opened the door to the passenger side. Underneath the driver's seat, my hand wrapped around cold steel. I crawled out of the pickup, released the safety and fired a shot into the air so Scott would know I was armed. I ran back and dove behind the car.

"Bob!" I said. He was slumped against the car, his eyes closed. I grabbed Bob's arm. "That smell!" I said.

"Gasoline," Bob said, his eyes had opened to slits. "He's going to burn us."

I crawled to the front of the car where I could aim over the hood. I peeked over the hood and saw Scott close to the church, a red gas can and the gun on the ground beside him. He threw a match at the church. It sputtered out and he tried to light another. He was trying to burn the church.

I lined up the sights and shot the gas can. Scott shrieked and threw the matches. The gas can made popping sounds and flew back towards me. It landed just on the other side of my car. Scott ran for his car and I ducked back down by Bob.

A motor gunned to life and I breathed a sigh of relief when I heard Scott's car turn onto the road and accelerate. "He's gone," I said. Bob was still slumped against the car, his chin resting on his chest. His eyes were closed. "We're going to be okay," I said as a small pop followed by a crackling sound came from the other side of my car. The gas can had caught fire. I dropped the gun, grabbed Bob under the arms and drug him into the cemetery. I propped him against a headstone and heard a loud whoosh.

My car was on fire. No explosion, just the whole car up in flames. I heard a siren coming closer. "Help is nearly here," I said to Bob.

Bob still didn't answer. I felt for a pulse and couldn't find one. I checked to see that he was still breathing. "Hold on, just hold on," I said to him as Newt's car pulled up, followed by the Bend Brook Rescue Unit. I waved my arms to the rescue unit and soon Harvey, the EMT from the previous night, came into the cemetery with a first aide kit.

"He's still breathing," I said. "But he doesn't have a pulse! What do we do now?"

Harvey knelt down beside Bob and listened to his chest. "We let him go," he said.

Sid and I were sitting in the back of a patrol car, a fire engine was parked in front of us. Bob's body was being brought out from the cemetery on a gurney, to be loaded into the ambulance parked in back of us. I looked over at my former car. It had burned down to the wires in the seat cushions. At least the volunteer fire department had gotten there before the church had caught on fire.

"Thanks for the info," Sid said into his cell phone. He snapped the phone shut and wrote something in his notebook.

A state trooper looked in the open window at Sid. "Is that Sid Weissman?" he asked.

"In the flesh," Sid answered.

"Word on the street is that you retired," he paused. "At least that was the word ten, maybe twelve years ago."

"What's the matter with you?" Sid asked.

"There's nothing the matter with me," the trooper replied indignantly.

"There must be something that matter with you that you ain't never heard of a cold case cop." Sid said.

The trooper pulled on the front brim of his hat and chuckled. "You're so full of it, Weissman."

"I cleared six cases this week, how about you?" Sid said.

"You did not clear six cases," the trooper said.

Sid pointed the pen at me. "Ask her how many cases I cleared."

"Six," I said.

"And that call just now?" Sid said. "It was from the Kansas Highway Patrol to let me know they pulled Scott Torrance over just outside of Marysville."

"They have him?" I asked.

Sid's thin lips curled into a smile. "Girlfriend, he's going down."

THIRTY

It was pouring rain on Monday morning. Since I didn't have a car, Clint dropped me off at the courthouse. I settled in at my desk and was flipping through my Rolodex to find Mary Lee's number when Dot came in and sat down. I glanced at her and when she didn't speak, I initiated the conversation. "What do you want?"

"We've run into some problems with the vegetable exchange."

"We?" I asked. I pulled out a notebook and pen and doodled in the corner.

When she didn't continue, I looked up to see she was biting her lower lip. "What is it?" I asked.

"Well," she paused.

"Spit it out, Dot," I said.

She gathered her self up. "Newt wants his table back."

We both looked over to the bedraggled table that held the vegetables.

"He's concerned . . ." she stopped.

"That I won't give back his table? That's ridiculous." I said. "He can have it."

"No, he's concerned about you. Haven't you heard? Karl Kittman said he's going to start a recall petition to remove Newt as Sheriff," she said.

I shrugged. "That has nothing to do with me," I said.

"Karl said you should be the next Sheriff and Newt's afraid you'll campaign when people bring in vegetables," Dot said.

I shook my head. "I'm not campaigning."

She still sat there, biting her lip. "You might not even have to campaign," she said. "But let me tell you, if things had turned out differently and the church would have burned instead of your car . . ."

"Dot!" I said. "I don't want to be Sheriff. I'm not qualified to be Sheriff."

Dot exhaled. "Well, I'm glad to see you've retained at least a little bit of common sense."

I tore a sheet of paper off the notepad and balled it up to throw it in the wastepaper basket. "Was that all?" I asked.

"Well, no. We also have another problem with the vegetable exchange."

"We?" I asked.

"The temperature is this room is just beyond control, and we can't leave the air conditioner on overnight. With zucchini season on us and the tomatoes starting to turn, we're going to have to discontinue the vegetable exchange."

There was a tap at my door. We turned to see Doris standing there. "Come in," I said.

"I'll tell Newt he can come get his table," Dot said. She got up and walked out.

"Is this a bad time?" Doris asked.

"Not at all," I said. "What's on your mind?"

"Wendell called," she said, smiling. "He's coming back! At least temporarily since the judge asked him to be a special prosecutor in the Coffers case."

"Oh, good," I said.

"And he wanted me to check with you," she said.

"Check with me about what?" I asked.

"He said when you were having lunch with him last Friday, you just bolted after he started discussing the Coffers case. He said if he takes this case, he's already decided he'll ask for probation for Mitch Banner and he doesn't want anyone making a fuss like he had to deal with before, so he wanted me to check with you first," she said.

"I wouldn't make a fuss," I said.

"I did tell him not to take the lunch personally. I told him that you'd nearly fainted dead away on Friday night," she said. "And I told him you had quite the eventful weekend," she added, "what with your car burning up and all."

I doodled on my calendar wondering where Jessica and Logan were at the moment. "I think it would be good if Wendell took the case," I said. "He's already familiar with it."

"That's exactly what I thought, too," she said. "Now, I see you have someone else waiting so I'll just run back downstairs and give him a call."

Mary Lee Parker stood in the doorway, an umbrella in one hand and her brown satchel in the other. Rain dripped from her rain coat and her umbrella. With the dour expression on her face, she reminded me of a demented Mary Poppins.

I stood up in my chair, "Mary Lee," I said. "I've been waiting to hear from you! How are Jessica and Logan?"

She remained standing in the doorway. "I've had a hellish weekend. Jessica tried to run Saturday night and I'll have you know," she slid out of the rain coat, "I spent most of my day off yesterday imploring that child not to do anything stupid."

"Why would she run?" I asked "What happened?"

"The family is not set up for toddlers," she stepped into the office. "Logan wouldn't stay in bed and the other kids were complaining about him. Jessica was slipping out a window with Logan when she was caught."

I bit my lip. "Could they have a bedroom to themselves?" I asked. "If they could have a bedroom to themselves, I'm sure that wouldn't have happened."

"Not at that home." Mary Lee shook herself off and sat in the chair in front of my desk, her bottom lip starting to quiver. "I do have another place in mind. I think she'd stay. They're a nice couple," she said.

"Have you asked them?"

Mary Lee leaned across the desk. "I'm asking right now," she said.

"Clint and I?"

"I've already called to make sure Clint's fingerprints for the criminal history check are processed today," Mary Lee said, sitting down. "That and some paperwork are the only things keeping you and Clint from being foster parents."

"But did we pass the home visit?" I asked. "Coco snapped at the woman who came to our house."

"Get a leash," Mary Lee said. "Gillian, do you want to be a foster mom to both Jessica and Logan, or not?"

I thought about it for a second. I did want them. Very much. "Yes," I said to Mary Lee. "I want them both." I called Clint at work and explained what was going on. "He'll be here in five minutes," I said as I hung up the phone. "He's taking the rest of day off so he can get the house ready. How soon will we get them?"

"We need to finish the paperwork. Maybe this afternoon if everything goes as it should." Mary Lee stood up. "Gillian," she said, "congratulations. You are about to have a boy, and a girl." She picked up the dripping brown satchel and I pushed aside papers as Mary Lee's briefcase came down in the middle of my desk.

LaVergne, TN USA
04 December 2009
165988LV00004B/4/P